Walls

An Ursula Nordstrom Book

HARPER & ROW, PUBLISHERS

NEW YORK

Cambridge
Hagerstown
Philadelphia
San Francisco

London
Mexico City
São Paulo
Sydney

1817

Jay Daly **Walls**

Walls

Library of Congress Cataloging in Publication Data
Daly, Jay.
  Walls.

  "An Ursula Nordstrom book."
  SUMMARY: Frankie O'Day, an incurable graffiti writer,
has to deal with pranksterish friends, an alcoholic
father, and a new romance.
  I. Title.
PZ7.D16956Wal   1980   [Fic]   79-2020
ISBN 0-06-021392-2
ISBN 0-06-021393-0 lib. bdg.

FIRST EDITION

FOR MY MOTHER

There is nothing worse for mortal man than wandering.

Odyssey 15:343

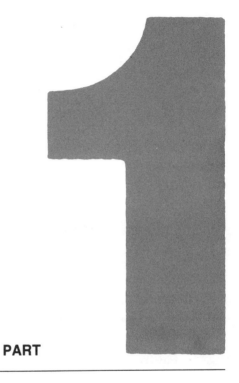

PART

God is great
God is good
Let's clean up
the neighborhood
    —the shadow

Frankie twisted the plastic cap over the wet end of his
white marker and stepped back to gain perspective on

his verse. The thin white paint was streaky over the dark lacquer of the mahogany church door, but the words were legible enough. Behind the door an organ moaned, keeping lethargic time with the wedding ceremony being enacted within. Pledges of eternal love and devotion. And fidelity. Meanwhile, outside, Frankie had written something a little more reasonable on the door.

> Let's clean up
> the neighborhood

Start with the door.

He danced down the church steps, his sneakers quiet and deft over the ancient stone. Skipping from the sidewalk across the deserted street, he stopped by the nearest lamppost and waited. The wedding ritual lumbered on; Frankie lit a cigarette and looked at the steeple. Striving toward God, he thought, like all of us, hoping we're pointed in the right direction.

What was it his father had said the other night? Cultivate your bubble. That was it, cultivate your bubble. Frankie smiled to himself and shook his head. It was good advice, if a little oddly put, particularly considering the source. His father had a more fragile bubble than perhaps anyone he could think of. It required much care. But at least it was his own, made by himself, and not something bought and fitted for him in Ghirardelli Square. Or at Neiman-Marcus.

Frankie dragged on the cigarette and tasted the burnt tobacco with his tongue. Reacting to the smoke, his stomach rumbled horribly, reminding him he'd had nothing to eat that morning, nothing at all but a cup of instant coffee which hadn't even completely dissolved in the hasty tepid water. Unsightly freeze-dried particles floated lazily on the brown liquid like islands of ash in a rotten volcano. It was disgusting, and clearly not the way to start this new, bright, rather auspicious day, but it was all he'd had at the time. And you had to work with what you had; that was the first lesson: Cultivate your bubble.

His stomach rumbled again, with patient and seemingly endless flatulence, still working on the wretched coffee. It must have been the brand, Bleak House, with its picture of a nineteenth-century waif stencilled on the front, holding a tin cup beneath his ravaged, desperate face. Feed me! Whose idea was that?

A small contingent of capped and liveried men came into view from behind the church. The drivers, of course, just back from a smoke or from a quick game of craps in the churchyard. He'd forgotten about them—good thing they hadn't caught him at his work, not that they could have done much. The Shadow could have outrun that group on all fours.

The organ groaned to a stop, and the ceremony shifted gears into a more silent, irrevocable phase.

Frankie O'Day, a.k.a. (or rather a.n.k.a., also not known as) The Shadow, phantom kamikaze vandal and defiler of virgin surfaces, took another casual drag and watched the drivers climb into their limousines. They looked bored. Just outside their very limited sphere of notice stood The Shadow, unknown and entirely new to them, and he was at that very moment considering the exquisite merit he might derive from writing on their cars. While they sat bored within. How about:

> Next stop, General Hospital

or,

> The bride is pregnant
> The groom is impotent
> The milkman is leaving on the next bus

or, if this seemed a bit juvenile, and it did, then something heavier,

> What convenience hath joined together . . .

put that on the first car, then

> Let convenience only put asunder

on the second.

It was all idle speculation, though, because the character of sound from within the church indicated that there was probably not much time to go before the wedding party emerged and all present burst into an orgy of confetti throwing, littering the sidewalk for an entire block. There was already a rumbling and scuffling noise from inside.

The wedding party burst from the church amid a cloud of rice, confetti, and whatever other trash might be thrown to stimulate the fertility of the exiled couple. Nowadays they should throw pills and diaphragms and condoms, but old traditions die hard. They went through their sidewalk celebrations, the waving and crying, kisses for the bride and obscene suggestions for the groom, before the whole group piled into their cars and rolled slowly away. Only the young preacher remained behind, like someone whom they'd planned to take and had forgotten. The soft wind blew confetti in the street.

Frankie was turning to leave as the thin, sickly cleric mounted the stone stairs to return to the church. His eyes must have adjusted slowly, through his glasses, but finally he realized the vision which the church door presented him and he hopped into a flurry of disjointed motion. Flinging open the door, he shuffled madly into the empty church yelling, "Rev-rund! Rev-rund Slocum! Rev-rund!"

The slick brown door closed deliberately behind him, as he disappeared into the holy caverns. "Revrund!" The door clicked shut, preserving his cry, like that of a wounded animal, in the hollow darkness.

Frankie O'Day was sixteen years old, would be seventeen in September, had been writing on the sides of buildings and things under the nom de plume of The Shadow for about three years, since beginning high school, had been playing basketball for many years longer than that, had been voted all-city in his junior year, went to Loyola High School, a Jesuit high school in the Sunset district of San Francisco, would probably get a basketball scholarship to someplace after his senior year, probably USF at least, where he knew the coach, or rather where the coach knew him, was six feet four inches tall, with longish brown hair and brown eyes and thick Mick Jagger-type lips (which they said he got from his father) but rather retiring ways really and he was the type who really never wanted to hurt anyone's feelings, such as the young cleric's for example, but who did at times because it was really very very difficult (impossible?) to predict just what the results of one's actions might be upon someone else. It was just very difficult to tell.

Frankie's father had been a very promising architect (considered quite clever and innovative) in the fifties. He and his young wife had travelled a year in Europe, on a liberal fellowship, observing buildings and washing themselves with that European style and elegance, just lately retrieved from the horror of war. This had all occurred before Frankie was born, but he felt he could picture them somehow, walking hand in hand through the streets of Paris and staring up, with a shared satisfaction, at the figured spires of some ancient cathedral. It was a picture in hazy black and white, as if drawn from the depths of a completely forgettable movie he might have seen in his youth. In fact it probably was, but that didn't change either the romance of the scene or his utter belief in its truth.

His father had begun drinking heavily when Frankie was very young. He remembered it as a gradual thing, from drink to more drink to more drink, and so on. At last it came upon him fully, and by that time Frankie had come to accept it, as children accept many things, as if it had always been there.

It was difficult to say what it was that had provoked all that drinking in the first place. Some forgotten slight, or half-forgotten disappointment. No one knew, or seemed to care. What mattered was that he was gone, not that he had been driven to it, if indeed he had been. For all they knew, it might have been fate.

Frankie had been looking for a stapler once, to join together two dissimilar pieces of homework, when he'd come across a carbon of an old letter in a bottom drawer. It was a copy of an application his father had made for a teaching position at the UC Berkeley School of Architecture. It listed his achievements, small but promising, and his references, now forgotten. The final paragraph was the most painful for Frankie to read. The business-letter officiousness seemed like a cover. Underneath there were signs of fear from one who feels something slipping fast away from him.

> . . . Although I have done nothing since the Baxter House, it is not for lack of trying, nor for lack of ideas. In fact, it is my design which was used in the superstructure of the Oakland Palladium, although I received no actual credit for the project. I would be most happy to bring a selection of my recent material for your inspection to any interview you may wish to arrange.
>
> Looking forward to hearing from you, I am
>
> > Sincerely,
> > F. X. O'Day

Frankie had read the letter and felt the weight of knowledge in his heart. He'd never got the job. What had happened? What reply had the letter prompted?

Had his father's confidence been already eroded by the uncaring world, or was this rejection among the first to drive him toward his alcoholic exile? He'd asked his mother about it once, when they were alone, but she had only shaken her head and told him that, as far as she could remember, there had never even been such an application. It must have been just some scrap paper he'd used and discarded. No, it couldn't have been very important at all.

It might just as well have been fate that caused him to drink.

In later years, Frankie thought he recognized the sad futility of his father's gesture. He hadn't been in their league—he must have known it at the time—yet he'd sent off his application anyway. Why had he humiliated himself like that?

Your father is a brilliant man, his mother had always said, brilliant. But then, she said more or less the same thing about Frankie. Probably he and his father were very much alike, not in the brilliance his mother spoke of, but in their damning just-above-averageness. That would be their cross to bear. That was why Frankie had found himself blushing as he read his father's letter. And that must also have been the root cause of his father's drinking. Great expectations.

Well, either that or it might have been fate.

His mother had wanted to be a lawyer all her life. She had begun her study at one time and broken it off, to get married Frankie always thought (although she assured him that her decision had been made much earlier), but she returned to it later, after Frankie had reached school age. And—more to the point—after his father had begun his drinking.

Frankie remembered the early years of uncertainty, of being afraid to bring friends home, afraid of what they might see, and of what they might later say to the others. And there was always that weird, isolated feeling when you come to know that all the neighbors talk about you among themselves, sometimes even in your presence, with the tone of self-righteous contentment which great pity affords.

"That's the O'Day boy there. It's a crime, isn't it, the way his father is these days. I feel so very sorry for that boy. I don't know what's to come of him."

What did they think would happen? He grew up.

But there were other factors to contend with. For one thing, he loved his father. He couldn't understand so much of the prejudice. His father was never nasty or vicious, like so many other people. He never yelled or sang or hit his mother or any of those things drunks are supposed to do, according to the image. He never did anything. He sat around and watched TV, like an invalid. Sometimes he smiled. He always thanked you and smiled when you brought him something. He never argued, he never did anything. It was as if he had nothing left inside him, no strength, no frustrations, no plans, no disappointments, nothing.

He seemed to plan his life so as to take from his drinking the gentlest death he could manage. Sure he was self-destructive, maybe pathetic, but Frankie could think of people a lot more harmful, a lot more undeserving of this earth's space than he. And that was about all he ever took from the earth, its space.

Sometimes he was a problem, but not often. Once Frankie and a friend, Bobby Maher, had to carry him up a flight of stairs and put him to bed. It wasn't often that he brought friends home, but this time he had and they'd found his father on the landing between the first and second floors flat on his back, with his arms and legs spread out wide and his mouth open. He looked like a dropped egg on toast. They tried to wake him but he was a bit beyond that so they worked together to carry him up to the apartment. His mother opened the door for them and the three of them, leaning together, lugged him in to the bed, where he uncoiled into a position similar to that in which they'd found him. His mother had said nothing, nor had he, during the entire maneuver. When it was completed, they shut the door to the bedroom and went about their business, his mother to her study and he and Bobby to the living room to watch TV. Bobby never mentioned the incident, but slowly he and Frankie drifted apart. They weren't really that close to begin with.

But his father rarely needed that sort of assistance. He could take care of himself; he could manage on his own. Lately, though, he'd been going out less and less, preferring the dark living room and the television set, and Frankie thought that it was probably just as well.

His mother was the lawyer. Margaret O'Day, called Peggy by her friends, she was never anything but Pearl to her husband. "Thanks, Pearl dear. Love you, Pearl?" "You, too, dear." He would smile then and lapse peacefully into silence.

Margaret O'Day worked for a firm downtown that

specialized in civil rights cases but had managed to accumulate a goodly amount of money and prestige nevertheless. She spent a great deal of her time at the office, or in her study, working on her cases. The study was a small, musty room, made smaller by the four walls tiered with books, long endless rows of books bound in stodgy green, brown, and maroon. Her square table stood at the center of the room, three feet from the bookshelves on all sides, and it was permanently littered with open books and dry, stained coffee cups and ashtrays. There was one Spartan fold-up chair, which his mother moved to the different sides of the table, following the trail of her research as it led her. The room was always stale with the smoke and the intensity that she'd left there.

She was happy in her work; she drenched herself with it. When the offer came to join the firm downtown, Frankie thought he'd never seen her so exuberant, so alive. She flashed about that paralyzed apartment like a wind through a crypt, tossing things here and there, stirring inanimate objects into bright activity, spraying energy like an Irish setter just emerged from the ocean.

Her big chance, so to speak, came when she assumed control of the Ashad Atman case. It was a liberal's plum, and yet she, the only over-forty junior woman lawyer in town, had somehow wangled it for her very own. The eyes of the legal world were watching.

Atman was a sharp, distant, Muslim soul who had become something of a hero in the Fillmore district for his work with the lost and disaffected elements of the populace. He had been a midwife at the birth of numerous community programs and a bulwark against the menace of termination by hostile bureaucratic forces. Kids loved him. Mothers and grandmothers praised God for his existence.

Then came suddenly the news from Omaha, Nebraska, that Atman was wanted there on charges of rape and attempted murder. Everyone screamed. They couldn't believe it. All the notable spokespeople rallied to his defense. Most of them had never even seen him, much less worked with him, but they knew their constituents, and they knew which side of the bread carried their political butter, so their voices were heard. Counselor O'Day grabbed the case, like a cornered lioness, and the fight was on.

She began by fighting extradition. The governor seemed to be wavering, so she took her appeal to the people. The newspapers gave her a headline:

ATMAN VOWS TO FACE CHARGES IF NECESSARY

They appeared together in the bleached color of the TV news shows. The cameras and lights trembled, as if from the force of her conviction, as she spoke of their faith and honor. Atman stood silently beside her. The camera swooped and careened around him, but his implacable face showed no sign of notice. Peggy O'Day's thin voice cried out through the confusion.

Even Frankie, who was rarely moved to a political sentiment, found time to scrawl his own straw of protest on a plywood barrier at Market and Hyde, near the Civic Center.

Atman is you
Don't let him down
Cause if you do
I hope your teeth turn brown
—the shadow

It wasn't much but it was all he could think of at the time.

Slowly, things started changing. You could almost feel the public sentiment swelling in his favor. At last came the news from the governor's office that he would refuse to grant extradition. His grinning crusader's face filled all the media as the news was announced. California, and particularly San Francisco, was once again in the vanguard of the struggle for human dignity.

The O'Day household was in chaos, but an enjoyable chaos it was. Phones ringing madly, doorbell bonging endlessly, there was a succession of well-wishers who came to pay their respects. Gray, dignified lawyers came, like rosy, fat suitors, with expensive briefcases and imported shoes. They gave her gifts of compliments like boxes of candy to a schoolgirl, and his mother beamed with happiness.

Frankie would sit, amid all the confusion, and watch Atman, who smiled and replied when spoken to, but who otherwise remained impassive and aloof. His dark, craggy face was ageless, as if it had always looked the same and always would. Frankie had never been truly comfortable with him, and relaxed only when they'd made their good-byes and the door closed softly behind him. Even then, the mysterious smell of his leather jacket stayed behind for hours to haunt him.

Much of the hectic celebration died down after a while and left only the warm sense of victory, of satisfaction. It was during this most vulnerable time that the governor betrayed them. He went on TV, without warning to Atman or his attorney, and announced that he had been given information which seemed to indicate that it would be better for Atman to go through with the judicial process and to prove his innocence. Therefore, he had reversed his earlier decision and had just finished talking to the governor of Nebraska, telling him that they were now prepared to cooperate with the extradition. Then he wished Atman the best of luck.

Frankie's mother sat in silence as she watched. When it was over, and she'd recovered enough to move, she rushed to the phone to call Ashad. Her face was worried, as if she realized that he would need her behind him now more than ever.

She stood listening for some time, with the phone tight against her face. He never answered. Nor did she see him again.

As days went by, the papers came out more and more against him. They almost stamped him guilty; why else had he skipped? Frankie sadly agreed. Deep inside he'd always feared that Atman had been capable of anything, from the worst evil to the most sublime good. He was not an ordinary man.

His mother retreated from it all to her study. Nothing would ever again in this world excite her so much. The smoke thickened over the cracked spines of the lawbooks and her life went on.

One afternoon, when Frankie was standing down

by Fisherman's Wharf waiting for a bus, he heard two men in pin-striped suits discussing the case. They seemed to get a big kick out of it. One of them mentioned his mother and the other said, "Well, what did you expect? Look, she was giving him a helluva lot more than just legal advice and he even ran out on her." Both men shook their heads and chuckled.

Frankie stood looking at them for a long time. He felt paralyzed, empty. He thought of his mother's tired, worn face, and her quiet sadness. The fat, pink faces of the businessmen went on chuckling and Frankie could think of nothing but smashing them, beating the self-satisfaction out of them with a series of heroic rights and lefts. But each time he might have moved, the image of his mother's thin, all-too-real face intervened, and it washed all emotion from him but that of sadness. He loved his mother very much, it was a part of him. He loved her for what she was.

His bus came then, and he took his sweet time getting on.

Frankie had always been a fairly good student. He'd always thought he'd be better; after all, he was close to the smartest kid in his grammar school. His mother had succeeded in convincing him of that. If there was one thing she'd done wrong, one thing he might blame her for, it was her blind and absolute insistence upon his superiority. Finally, she even infected Frankie with this dangerous attitude. Thus, it came as quite a shock when he entered high school and the walls of his private monument disintegrated before the unguessed harsh reality of his experience. Loyola drew from the whole city. It gathered a crowd of minor neighborhood geniuses and dropped them together like a flock of neurotic roosters in a concrete ring. Naturally, most of them fell apart. As far as Frankie was concerned, it certainly knocked him for a loop, it certainly did. He just wasn't prepared for it. As a result, his most secret reaction was one of defense. He'd been hurt, despite his mother's confidence, and he resolved that it should never happen again, not if he could prevent it. From then on, if he had any monuments to cherish at all, he'd treat them carefully. At least until he was damn sure they could stand on their own.

Loyola was a venerable Jesuit institution, in strong Franciscan territory. The principal's name was Father Bulger. He was a big, strapping, aptly named man who wore his white hair in a crew cut and his face in a permanent scowl. It was not known for sure that Father Bulger was the toughest priest in the place, but it was strongly suspected, since there were some pretty tough cookies who were known to bend to his will. But then he was the principal.

St. Ignatius lived in a bust over the door, and probably in the hearts and minds of some of his teachers, too. At one time the teachers had all been priests, but now there were three civilians for every priest, and their ratio seemed destined only to increase. Sign of the times.

Loyola was all boys, of course, and that may have been a part of the reason that the school was blessed with a perennially superior basketball team. None of its alumni had ever gone on to play in the pros, but many had graduated to fine careers in the college ranks. And some at least had gone to camp with a pro team, although all had been cut before the season started. Frankie had no illusions of his ever breaking the tradition, but he did expect his basketball to get him to college at least. And that was well within the tradition.

Life at Loyola was not hard, particularly if you played basketball. There was the letter, the large golden L, on your maroon-and-gold jacket. It was enough; nothing more was required to justify your existence. Not that Frankie was satisfied with such distinction—it was important only in that it met minimum requirements. Wearing the letter, he knew he was adequately defined and people would more or less leave him alone. In fact, with his letter, and with his ability to actually spell words correctly, Frankie found he was an unusual commodity on campus, the well-rounded man. Which sounded to him like nothing, the well-rounded onion.

That was when he began writing on walls, at Loyola. It may have been the walls, themselves, they were so powerfully there. The whole building was nouveau concrete, sprung up from the dirt beneath like a massive monument to the vision of the fifties. Inside, the concrete cinderblocks were painted pale green or beige or even gray, all fine institutional colors, but so bland and untainted in their brittle roughness that they seemed to cry out for something to spark them to life. This, Frankie felt, he had provided.

He still remembered his first attempt, written with

a crumbling black crayon on the light-brown wall leading to the gym.

> **Mr Cruikshank is gay**
> —the shadow

From the very first he was The Shadow. Mr. Cruikshank was a gym teacher, hopelessly effeminate, who was known to spend inordinate periods of time folding sweatsocks in the freshman shower room.

Perhaps it wasn't the most imaginative thing he could have written, but it was something. What was more interesting was the reaction he drew from the normally apathetic (often half-stoned) student body. People actually talked about it (he heard them) and he was able to keep to himself, in a personal conspiracy, his delight at the whole idea. It was a new excitement; he felt like The Scarlet Pimpernel or someone, an agent of discord behind enemy lines.

Someone finally erased that one, using soap and hot water, but they left behind a circular patch of white on the darker wall to remind everyone of The Shadow's presence.

Frankie kept on writing then, mostly innocuous things about Mrs. Cram, who was the school librarian and the only woman in the area save Miss Isaacs, who was the gray-haired secretary in the office. Other circles of lighter shade then began to appear, like magic haloes in the dry concrete. And The Shadow's mystery grew.

"Who is this Shadow, anyway?"

"Look, I don't know for sure, but I hear it's that kid Frazier over in B-7."

"Frazier?"

"Yeah. You know, the kid with the red hair."

"Frazier, yeah, Frazier. Is that who it is?"

"That's right."

"Did they catch him or something?"

"Not yet."

"Man, I'd hate to be in his shoes when they do."

"Yeah, they'll probably all take him out back and beat the shit out of him."

"I know it, and charge him for a paint job, too."

"Yeah."

"Hey, wait a minute. Frazier. Frazier. Is that Billy Frazier?"

"Right."

"Wasn't he the one who got arrested for stealing that car?"

"Right."

"Yeah, well, I've heard of dumber things, but driving a stolen car at eighty miles an hour the wrong way on the Golden Gate Bridge is about as insane as you can get."

"Yeah, the bastard is definitely crazy, there's no doubt about that."

"It's too bad."

"What's too bad?"

"Didn't you hear? He's getting thrown out of school. I think he's already gone."

"No kidding?"

"That's right."

"Wow."

"No more Shadow."

"Yeah, right. Unless it's not him."

"Yeah."

Frankie didn't mind that a succession of others kept getting credit for his work. In fact, he rather enjoyed it. Most of them would deny it when asked, but who wouldn't? Admitting it would have been plain crazy, or suicidal at best. Some didn't exactly deny it, but they would refuse to comment, or something equally silly, and these, Frankie decided, were the future suicidal types anyway.

Meanwhile, The Shadow continued his work, unobserved and unsuspected. His messages began to reflect a concern with greater things, heavier concepts.

Blessed are the rich, for they shall buy happiness
—the shadow

Blessed are the meek, for the rich shall step on them
—the shadow

Blessed are those who beat up young boys,
for they shall see God
—the shadow

Blessed are those who are beaten for education's sake
for they shall grow up
to kick the shit out of their teachers' grandchildren
—the shadow

For the most part, Frankie shied away from obscenities in his writing. He didn't feel that it was fitting. As his work progressed, though, he did find the need to sneak one in here and there, just for emphasis. Once, though, he had let his emotion get the better of him and he wrote simply,

Fuck!
—the shadow

His mistake should have been immediately apparent, but it wasn't, until he saw the wall the next day. Beneath his exclamation someone had written

I'd love to
—Mr Cruikshank

Frankie felt the heat of his blood flooding his face. He felt strangely violated. It was another scribbler, invading his special world. He should have known, it was inevitable, but it still came as a shock. Even worse was his schizophrenic anger that it was The Shadow's integrity, not Frankie's, which had been sullied by this foreign hand. He stomped away to think, to plan somehow for the defeat of this pretender.

The funny thing was that everyone loved it. They thought it was the funniest graffiti yet. Most of them assumed that The Shadow had written the whole dialogue, an assumption which Frankie thought most unperceptive. It gave him an unhappy insight into the level of sophistication of his audience. Still, something had to be done. He finally got the idea in, of all places, history class. Late that afternoon, when the halls were deserted, he added another line, in a strong, boxlike printing.

If you wish to converse with me, define your terms
—the shadow

Well, that stopped everyone. There was simply no reply to that, nothing that could safely be put on a wall at least. Perhaps his adversary considered doing some sort of definition but he never did. Nor did he ever again risk badinage with The Shadow. Frankie stood alone, and invisible, at the top.

He slipped into high gear after that. His first objective was to absolutely madden the administration while remaining undetected and serene in his person. He succeeded. Even while they were tearing their hair out and subjecting every troublemaker within five miles to the third degree, The Shadow's messages appeared miraculously on the barren walls.

One which gave him special pleasure, because of its length and its source, went up in blazing Day-Glow orange on the dark wood just outside the chapel.

> If the whole society
> should come to an end
> It would take me fifteen minutes
> to regain my composure
> —the shadow

It took them about fifteen hours to scrub that one off the wall, but it was a minor victory, since Frankie could tell by the comments he heard that most people hadn't the foggiest notion what he meant. They all liked the colors: bright orange over brown. Nor did anyone seem to recognize the irrepressible style of old Ignatius Loyola, famous madcap comedian and founder of schools for boys. Even the Jesuits didn't seem to recognize it.

On the other hand, the most notorious of his school graffiti was one which was seen by practically no one. It happened on a weekend, when school was closed and Frankie had sequestered himself, after basketball practice, in the weight room. The yearbook had just come out, bound in maroon and gold, with the graduation inscription printed in raised script across the front cover. It was the yearbook motto that caught his eye, and it was in French. *Simple et sans foi comme un bonjour.* Nobody knew what it meant, and nobody cared. Underneath was printed the name of the man who had had this deathless thought: —*Laforgue.* It was a brilliant, unconscious parody of The Shadow himself! Obviously an opportunity not to be wasted.

He had no pens with him, but he did have a small jacknife. He took it with him up the stairs to the office. On the main door, brown and silent, was the nameplate, REV. E. J. BULGER, S.J. The Shadow scraped his message through the dark stain to the white wood beneath.

Simple et sans foi comme un Bulger
—the shadow

Someone found it first thing Monday morning and had the door removed from its hinges and taken to the shop to be refinished. In the time it was off, Father Bulger was obliged to sit exposed, in plain view of the student body, his red face broiling under the familiar haircut, behind his overgrown, polished desk. Somehow, everyone soon knew that the missing door had been The Shadow's doing, and speculation raged as to what the offending message had been. Students paraded by the office, to have a look. For his part, Father Bulger was visibly harassed. He continued to do whatever kind of work Jesuit principals do, but every other minute he would look up to find curious students staring at him. Finally, he threw down his long dark pen and walked out, telling everyone in a loud voice that he would be back when the door was repaired.

The student body cheered mindlessly. Bulger had been driven out by The Shadow. Pandemonium.

Frankie had been there when he'd walked out and was a little surprised at the priest, at the way the whole thing had affected him. He really thought that Bulger would take it much better than he did. This wasn't the same Father Bulger who was famous for telling an irate parent (who had brought in a dentist bill resulting from a Jesuit backhand to his son's fragile bicuspid) to "take a walk. If you don't like our discipline here, then take your son out of school." He had definitely lost his composure over the incident of the door.

Despite the unanimous approval of the milling crowd of students, Frankie felt only that sudden sinking sensation in his stomach, that once again everyone was reacting entirely out of proportion to his intent. He stood gazing into that empty office and marvelled, not at his power, but at the ultimate uselessness of it all.

Things got hot at school after that one. There were secret meetings of the faculty and spies were appointed.

The message was clear: Get The Shadow. Priests and custodians, even lay teachers, began appearing in the corridors at odd hours. The word was out: The Shadow must be identified and rooted out, like a cancer in their midst. The nervous and timid students were grilled. Perhaps they gave some names, under pressure or panic, but none was ever the name of The Shadow. No one knew; it was as simple as that. What had started as a lark for Frankie had become, in the tumult of escalation, a habit, a trust. He took it more seriously than he might have predicted.

Also, it was a bit late for him to come forth and shout, "Okay, here I am, The Shadow, fooled ya, huh? Now let's forget the whole thing and go have a picnic."

No, that wouldn't do.

That wouldn't do at all.

What he could do, what he would have to do, was to cease and desist from his Shadow persona on the school property. The danger of exposure outweighed all personal advantage to be gained from continuing. The finality of the decision was accompanied by a strange nostalgia, as if a certain period of his life had drifted irretrievably from him. He could only stand and watch it receding in the distance.

But there was also a frontier feeling at that moment, like that of a self-conscious bird flung out of its familiar nest. There was a whole world out there to write on.

Even as The Shadow left, graduating reluctantly before the rest of his class, he knew he could not do so without ceremony. His answer came, once again, from the classics. Not to mention the orange spray can of Day-Glow paint, very effective:

> What is expressed is impressed
> —the shadow

He printed this parting message in heroic letters, almost as tall as himself, across the concrete facade of the school. It mocked and dwarfed the metal inset lettering above, **Loyola High School**. It made a fitting and just farewell for The Shadow, who left the school then, never to return. Frankie, of course, would be back for classes on Monday.

Everything was so much more complicated on the outside. It was a different world. There was competition, but it was so fragmented, so sloppy, that it did more to still his desire than to spark it.

> Power to the people!
> Boycott lemons!
> Free the buena vista 27!
> Anarchists unite!
> Red power!
> White power!
> Brown power!
> Gay power!
> Black power!
> Samoan power!
> Solar power!

It was as if the walls were screaming at him. Who needed all that noise? Even when the writing seemed to offer consolation it was usually a fake-out.

Have a nice day
Asshole

Sometimes there would appear a person who could actually put enough words together to form a complete sentence and would write something like

Sex is great over half the time
The other half is even better under

which seemed to Frankie clever, if a little confusing at first. It was better at least than the usual: phone numbers which promised a good time, or grotesque drawings of what he assumed were supposed to be sexual organs.

It was all such a maze of acronyms and cryptic sentiment that it really meant nothing in the end. In the bathrooms of North Beach bars you'd find things like

Wittgenstein was a pederast

which was probably some sign of intelligence but it did nothing for Frankie. Of course, he didn't know who the fellow was, so he might have missed the joke, but so what? It was all the same garbage as far as he was concerned.

There was really only one distinctive and repeated design which attracted him. It was all over the city, just one word, sprayed on walls with some kind of paint spray gun. The round red letters were always the same, like a recurrent challenge. The word was

action

in a mellifluous scrawl, blood red. Action, it was always the same. After you looked at it for a while, the word seemed to disintegrate into its constituent letters, so as to be almost unintelligible. Then it came together, after you shook your head, or stood back a ways. Action. It was hard to tell what the writer meant. Action. That's what made it so distinctive. It was head and shoulders above all the other junk that people had thrown on the city's walls. But it was the other junk, the utter volume of it, which had taken Frankie aback at first. He decided to start slowly.

> **The shadow lives!**
> —the shadow

which was followed by

> **The shadow knows!**
> —the shadow

which was when he started to lose control and wrote things like

> **The shadow craves affection!**
> —the shadow

and finally crazy screams like

> **Read me! Read me!**
> —the shadow

but it was clear at that point that he was definitely freaking out, so he stopped writing for some time to take stock.

If a thing was worth bothering to do at all, it should be done right. Just what was his objective?

He didn't know.

What was his style, his persistent message?

It wasn't clear.

Whom would he speak to, now that his captive audience at Loyola was gone?

He had no idea.

It was all very depressing then, when he realized this. Instead of moving up to the major leagues in a sweat of exhilaration and challenge, he seemed to have come to the ballpark and found it deserted, abandoned, grass growing untended in the dugouts.

Part of it was just a lack of ideas on his part. What the hell was there to say, anyway? Most of the things he'd done at Loyola were either copied from books, or local jokes, or just simple things whose existence was justified only by his ingenuity at getting them on the walls. There were times when he'd been able to deceive himself into thinking that his fellow students' appreciation for The Shadow was something other than their predictable merriment at a blackboard eraser tossed against a wall, or a phantom fart from the back of the class, but in his depression he was less able to see the difference. What was the sense in it all?

This frame of mind, unhealthy as it was, might have continued to his artistic demise, had it not been for a single spontaneous outburst of stolen chalk and tin door on the Sunday before the last week of school.

He'd been wasting time, late in the afternoon, at a poolroom out near the beach. After giving up on the poolroom and leaving through the back door, he stood for a while in a deserted parking lot, which stretched in uneven fashion about twenty yards until it died against the dull brick facade which was the rear wall of an old police station. Two or three injured police cars lounged between faded white stripes, their grills silent and docile against the old brick station wall. Frankie went over to investigate.

As he walked, the rapid dry clicking of the balls, and the grumbling of the voices, receded, until they no longer existed. Everything seemed so quiet, so dead, that he felt as if he were the only human on earth. His sneakers flipped out stones and pieces of crumbled asphalt as he walked carelessly among the forgotten cars. The whole world had been deserted in the dying sunlight.

The back door of the police station, stuck like a patch on the dirty brick wall, attracted his attention. It looked both clumsy and formidable. An army of rusted nails surrounded it on all sides. The dingy metal stood unadorned within the nails, as if it were quietly ashamed of its neglected condition.

The Shadow smiled; he would take care of that.

He felt the broken cylinders of chalk in his pockets and played with them as he thought. There was only one inspiration that came to mind. He felt a quick resurgence of energy as he wrote it all out.

> Help me
> please
> I don't want
> to kill
> again.
> —the shadow

He went to school the next day, resigned to going through the motions but still revitalized by his marks on the tin door. He planned to sneak by after school and see if the words were still there. Quickly he learned that he wouldn't have to bother.

Loyola was crawling with detectives, Humphrey Bogart types in wrinkled raincoats and sweat-stained hats. They were congregated around the office and there was police business on their minds. The rest of the student body was nonplussed, but Frankie was just amazed. They were after him!

And they were. The Search for The Shadow was on again. The same procession of nonconformists and misfits was called to the office, this time to be subjected to a more professional inquisition, by the S.F.P.D. Frankie's quickened heartbeat told him that for the first time he was actually scared. Suddenly all the police in the city would be out looking for The Shadow, as if he were the Zodiac killer or something. How had he got himself into all this?

They hadn't called him to the office on Monday, and he was slowly gaining a renewed confidence in his invisibility when his name was called late Tuesday afternoon. Frankie O'Day, wanted in the office please.

Father Bulger was behind his desk, and to his right, in the vinyl easy chair, sat an imposing detective in a giant pile of wrinkled tweed.

Father Bulger did the introductions. "Frankie, this is Officer Mulcahey of the San Francisco Police."

Mulcahey nodded; Frankie said hello.

The priest continued, "The police want to ask everyone a few questions about this Shadow person."

"Oh."

"Sit down, Frankie." He indicated the hard, straight-backed chair which marked the apex of the equilateral triangle that was so weighted down at their end.

The detective had said nothing. He regarded Frankie with an Irish squint, as if he knew something into which no one but he and the TV audience at home had the faintest glimpse. There was a short, meaningful silence before he spoke.

"Frank"—he moved only his mouth—"we know that one kid in this school has been writing things on walls and calling himself The Shadow."

Frankie agreed, but Mulcahey ignored the interruption.

". . . And we don't mind the perverted, disgusting things he's been writing . . ."

Perverted, disgusting things?

". . . but murder is something else again."

Murder?

"We don't care that he's a homosexual. . . ."

?

". . . We don't care that he has no respect for property. . . ."

Frankie felt numb. Was this a movie?

". . . We don't care what his mother does with her free time. But we do care about murder."

Frankie nodded. He wanted to escape from this nut at all costs.

"Now, Frank, look." The pile of tweed shifted slightly in its chair. "We know that this sickie either goes to this school or spends a lot of his time here. What we want to know is his name. You understand?"

"Sure."

"Okay."

Father Bulger shuffled some papers. Mulcahey spent some time preparing his pitch.

"Now, Frank. It happens that your name has been mentioned in connection with this Shadow thing."

Frankie just barely stifled a momentary panic. His name? Whom had they browbeaten for that? No one knew. He was sure of it, no one.

He tried to look surprised. "My name?"

"That is correct. Your name was given as a person who knows something very special about this whole affair. Something very special."

Something very special. What did that mean? How much did this Mulcahey character know?

Frankie stuttered, "I—I—I don't know what you mean."

"You don't?"

Mulcahey paused to let that sink in. Frankie attempted to prevent his internal confusion from reaching his face. Mulcahey just stared at him.

Frankie cleared his throat and spoke. "Ah, no, I really don't. Nothing more than everyone else knows."

"What does everyone else know?"

"Well, you know, the things on the walls and all that."

"The things on the walls?"

A light went on in Frankie's head. He was trying

to trap him. "The things on the walls around the school here. You know. The graffiti."

Mulcahey grunted. His detective's stare continued. Frankie felt as if he'd won a small victory in their cat-and-mouse game. The school was all he knew about, nothing outside, just the school. He returned to the part he was supposed to be playing.

"Honestly, really, I don't know who it was that gave you my name but I think he made some kind of mistake."

"You do, do you?"

"Yeah, really." Frankie was so wide-eyed and innocent he surprised even himself.

The detective switched his expression suddenly down and to the side, as if from disgust. He spoke rapidly. "Okay, Frank, this is getting us nowhere. You can go, go ahead, but I just want you to know that we already have a fair idea who this pervert is and we're going to be watching him. He'll give himself away. We know that, you know that. He'll give himself away."

Frankie agreed gladly, with a note of inevitability in his voice, "Yeah, I know. They always do, they always do."

"You bet they do, Frank, and if this Shadow knows what's good for him he'll come forward now and prevent all that unnecessary bloodshed."

Bloodshed?

Frankie hoped they didn't see him choke. As he got up he said, "Well, I really hope he does, uhm, and I'm sorry I couldn't help you out, you know?"

Mulcahey stared at him. His eyes wouldn't let

Frankie out of the room until he'd finished. "Maybe you'll help us out yet, Frank. You never know, do you?"

"No, I guess not."

His legs were weak as he left. This was the big leagues here. For God's sake, he was a fucking murder suspect! The urge was fantastic to run back in and plead for mercy, anything to relieve the pressure, but he couldn't. His palms were damp and he felt at once that he was now living on some wild precarious edge of existence which he had never known before. A wanted fugitive. A phantom celebrity in the annals of crime. Of course, he didn't really deserve the renown, nor did he particularly want it, but it was there. They would be watching him.

Father Bulger followed him out. When they were alone in the corridor, the priest glanced back once over his shoulder and then turned, speaking in a whisper. "Don't worry, Frankie, he's been saying that to everyone."

At the end of the week, with school out for the summer, Frankie might have slid into another spell of isolated depression had it not been for his small, unheralded introduction to Laurel.

PART

Lopez Market. It was the one lonesome store in an otherwise residential block. Even its name was misplaced, since it wasn't really a market at all, not entirely. It was presently more a hangout than anything else. There were tables and chairs to the left of the entrance, along with four booths attached to the gray wooden wall, and to the right were two aisles of market-type offerings, leftovers from an earlier heartland-of-America neighborhood. The cereal boxes were covered with gray dust an eighth of an inch thick. Who would buy them?

Lopez, himself, was a dark Anthony Quinn-type Mexican with slick gray-streaked hair and a thin mustache. He was always just barely in control of things around the store. His wife was short, round, and silent. She made tortillas and enchiladas and tacos that achieved a small fame in the mostly Anglo neighborhood. These you could get to go or to eat at a table in the store. Most people got them to go. The kids, who could rarely afford the Mexican food anyway, were more apt to order coffee and English muffins than anything else.

There were two Lopez girls, both in their teenage years, and their existence probably contributed something to the patience of their parents with the crowd of hangers-out. Either that or they were beyond caring, permanently addled by the smoke and the grease and the general chaos of their situation.

Inez Lopez was about Frankie's age, but was very chubby and hampered by her lingering Mexican accent. She always looked as if she were caught in a wild, wrenching craving for affection which would never be satisfied. Everyone felt protective of her, the last thing she wanted. Lupe, her sister, who was about thirteen or so, was just that: loopy. She was wild. Lupe Lopez, flying about town in stolen cars and filled to the gills with an overdose of any one of a variety of strange pharmaceuticals, that was the picture. No one felt protective of her, although she probably needed it more than her sister.

Lopez Market was just down the street from Frankie's place, and it was central enough to draw from the younger element of the entire area. It was a hangout.

During basketball season, Frankie's afternoons and evenings were usually too tied up to permit the kind of indolence one found at Lopez. During the summer, though, when there was nothing to do (other than his daily games on the Prayerbook court—which was a semihidden slab of concrete across from the Prayerbook Cross in Golden Gate Park—or his scribbling on hot walls), Lopez was as good a place as any to pass the time.

Everyone at Lopez knew he was an all-city forward at Loyola. It seemed to impress them as much as it impressed him. Everyone else on the first team was black, and they were all taller than he was, even the guards, so it was hard to think of himself as anything but the token honkie. After all, the *Chronicle* and *Examiner* both printed the selectees' pictures, in formation, on the schoolboy sports extra. I mean, you had to have a white face in there somewhere. That face was Frankie's.

Not that he didn't deserve it; he deserved it as much as anyone. So did perhaps five or ten other athletes in the city, black and white. It was a lot of shit. Most of the people at Lopez seemed to know this. It didn't bother Frankie and it didn't bother them.

What they didn't know about, though, was The Shadow. The subject had never even surfaced in any of the conversations at Lopez Market. Frankie never felt inclined to bring it up, either. When he thought about it, he wasn't quite sure what it was that kept him from revealing it. It was real, though, his hesitance, and it was related more to embarassment than to anything else he could think of. There was just no natural way to introduce the subject; nothing, at least, which seemed at all natural to him. It always seemed forced, as if he would be some rich kid trying to carry off friendship in a whirlwind of money. Besides, it was always better to be mysterious than to be obvious. Witness one of his inscriptions, scrawled on the side of the Bank of America over on Geary near the hospital:

> All knowing's having
> And to have is
> perhaps the unkindest way
> to kill
> —the shadow

He got that from some poet, but he believed it implicitly. It was better to inhabit your own world, and to have a little bit of yourself, than to be swallowed up whole by that swirling monster called The World. The Shadow would stay removed from that.

Of course, if they somehow discovered his identity on their own, that would be all right. There would be nothing at all wrong with that. In fact, that would probably be just what he wanted. Not right yet, but sometime in the future it would be just what he wanted.

The type of individual who frequented Lopez was

probably not destined for the society pages, himself included. There were two who were always there, like Scylla and Charybdis, sitting on the sidewalk at the corner of the building with their backs straight against the brick and their legs out straight on the gray concrete. These were Jimmy and Joey Lactus, twin brothers in all senses of the word. They were both downer freaks—Seconals and Nembutals and Tuinals and an occasional Quaalude extravaganza, when the time seemed right. They'd always have a can of beer just to prevent dehydration and, of course, they never moved. They were just always there. It was as if they'd managed to find a drugstore with delivery service. "Oh, Ralphie, would you please run this case of reds over to the Lactus twins please, it seems they're in danger of regaining consciousness. Thank you." Sometimes, when they did try to get up, invariably together, it was a scene straight out of Dante, weeping and groaning and holding each other as the world rolled in a blur around them. Where they went, no one knew. But they were tolerated.

Other illustrious callers included Billy Lyons, who was considered crazy by all, but whom Frankie liked, possibly because he had a kind of genuine flair about him which the others lacked. He didn't seem to care about anything. Consequently, he was free to do or not to do whatever he wanted. No one objected. Billy was also the one who had written KICK ME in shaving cream on the back of the cop who directed traffic during rush hour in Union Square, and got away with it. He was known to do things like that. He said it made life interesting, and Frankie guessed that it did. It did make life interesting. It was also why Billy was considered crazy by all, except Frankie.

Jeremy Taylor, who was another frequent visitor, was the resident expert on the opposite sex. Ass man, as he liked to hear himself termed. Frankie could see that his sea-green eyes were different from most, but he just couldn't understand their effect on the girls. He'd heard them whispering, almost in awe (of this numbskull?), ". . . And his eyes, they're so deep, they see right through you, they see right through you." Unreal.

There was Maureen Murphy, a really mysterious Irish girl. She had red hair and freckles, but everything she said to you was as sharp and dangerous as an Amazon spear. No one ever dared to be her lover and she really didn't seem to mind.

There were others, all of them probably forgettable and soon to be lost in the crowd. There was Bob Gatz, for example, whom everyone called The Hard-On, even the girls, although never to his face. There was no sexual connotation, really. It was just that his father, who was a football nut, had had him shot up with steroids at an early age so that he'd be big enough for the pros. He'd developed permanent bulges in rather odd places. Hard as a rock, though, old Bob would be out there every day, with his father, in a deserted field, practicing his three-point stance. Frankie used to watch them from afar. Bob would grunt down, almost petrified in his heavy pads and plastic body, waiting for his father to blow the whistle. When it came, Bob would lurch up, screaming like Frankenstein, run for about five yards, and fall spread-eagled on the dusty ground. Then he would struggle up for more. Frankie found the whole scene fairly offensive. When they were through, they'd retire to his father's station wagon, probably to prepare another shot. People sometimes laughed at Bob Gatz when he came into Lopez, called him The Hard-On, but that was one thing Frankie found he couldn't do. Everyone was also surprised when Bob Gatz made first-team all-scholastic at Polytechnical, but Frankie wasn't. He was just a little saddened by the whole thing.

Bob Gatz was there the day Laurel came. He was stuffed into a booth in the corner along with two other guys whose names Frankie didn't know. Everything was much as it had always been. The screen door flapped open and shut as people entered and exited and often reentered in their daily rounds. The closest conversation was among Billy Lyons, a kid named Bennie, and Maureen Murphy, who, as usual, was the instigator of the whole thing. She had casually mentioned that she had a tattoo of the Rolling Stones' tongue on her ass. The left cheek, to be exact.

"Oh, come on, Mo, you're shittin' me."

Maureen looked offended.

Bennie just shook his head.

Billy pressed the point. "Okay, Mo, so you got a tongue on your ass, big deal."

"I never said it was a big deal."

"Big deal."

"Big deal nothing. What've you got on your ass, Lyons?"

"A bunch of little hairs."

"Oh, that's exciting."

But Bennie was definitely inquisitive. "Can we see it?"

"Ha!"

"That's 'cause it's not there," Billy said.

Bennie looked disappointed.

Maureen was above it all. "There's no way a little twat like you would ever know if it was there or not."

"Why didn't you put it on your face?" asked Billy. "It looks like an asshole anyway."

Maureen leaned toward him. "Just because *you* don't know the difference doesn't mean other people don't."

"Oh, fuck you, Mo, the only way you'd get a tongue on your ass is to paint it there yourself."

The conversation proceeded along those lines, very typical and vulgar, while Frankie's mind wandered in the stagnant cage that was Lopez. Looking through the smoke, he glimpsed Pauline Alee and another girl through the hazy front window. They were approaching Lopez across the sunlight of the street. He knew Pauline, who was sometimes loud, but basically friendly. He didn't know the other girl; in fact, he'd never seen her before. She walked with Pauline like a fresh image, with her arms folded across her chest in that special, pensive, contained walk which only girls seem able to effect. Frankie felt his own breath flow out toward that figure from his first glimpse of her. It was a very personal thing.

They entered, standing for a long moment in the doorway, while the screen door bounced shut behind them. Pauline was short and very dark, with black hair and a kind of flat-footed dominance about her wherever she stood. But the other girl was brilliant. She stood beside Pauline like a spot of sunshine next to the shade. She was alive; he could tell. Taller than Pauline, she wore the same kind of outfit, jeans and a shirt, but her jeans seemed made for her body only and her shirt seemed just laundered and starched and placed upon her in such clean and careful style. Her clothes looked as if they'd never been worn.

Pauline and her friend approached the booths. The only space was directly across from Frankie, that having recently been vacated by two of the three barbarians who were arguing about tattoos and assholes.

"Hi, Frankie," said Pauline. "Can we sit down?"

"Sure."

Pauline stepped aside and ushered the new girl into the booth before taking her own place to the outside. Frankie adjusted himself in his seat, separated from them by the immovable bulk of the pitted wooden table.

"This is my cousin, Laurel Travers," Pauline announced.

Laurel said, "Hi."

"Hi."

"She's from L.A."

"No kidding?"

"Yeah. We just moved up."

"Great."

Frankie thought she was smiling at him with a special smile, much as his own smile was directed toward her. It was a stupid thing to think, there was nothing to indicate that her smile was anything other than her usual smile, but Frankie felt blessed nonetheless. And she did have a fantastic smile.

"How do you like our fair city so far?"

"Oh, I love it. I always have."

"How does it compare with L.A.?"

"They're—different," she said emphatically. "They're just entirely different. L.A. is bigger and sunnier and wilder, but San Francisco seems to have more—class, you know?"

"Yeah."

When she talked she made it seem like such an event. She didn't always look at him; in fact, her warm sloe eyes wandered habitually as she talked, up and around, as if they were a part of her communication. But when her statement was completed, her eyes always came back to him, and settled there, nestling against his own.

They were brown, her eyes, and they reminded Frankie of the eyes of someone famous, someone he couldn't quite identify. They were so unusual and quick that they immediately drew all attention to her face. The fragile, light-brown waves of her hair set them off, and her round blushing flower of a mouth was perfect beneath. Her cheeks seemed to have a natural flush, just like the cheeks of girls celebrated in song for hundreds of years. Frankie was struck by her movements as she spoke. It was all such an uncommon symmetry and grace gathered into one slight apparition. He felt so rough and earthbound by comparison.

They were interrupted then by the sound of Mr. Lopez chasing a dog out of his store. He waved his arms frantically and swore at the unfortunate animal in Spanish. Soon everyone in the store took up the chant, yelling unintelligible things at the bewildered dog. Lopez lunged toward it and opened the door behind with one motion of his outstretched arm. The dog took off, with a mock-heroic parting yelp, across the busy street and into the distance.

The whole place rocked with a shared laughter.

Frankie glanced over, as the hoopla subsided, and watched Laurel. She had turned her head to view the action and the upswept curve of her jaw toward her chin was so swift and fine through her white white skin that it lifted Frankie's breath right along with it. She was looking away and her mouth had relaxed, open, into a smile. Her lower lip was round and just barely moist. Her eyes darted back and forth, following her own curiosity in the laughing market.

Frankie's heart plunged suddenly with the knowledge. How could he ever ever have something as absolutely perfect as that?

But then she turned back to him, back to *him*, and she was smiling.

"What kind of group is this?" She laughed.

"Oh, just your usual group of 4-H club rejects," said Frankie.

"Who was the dog?"

"Who was the *dog*? I don't know. Whoever he was, he didn't know the password."

She tilted her head to the side. "And what is the password?"

Frankie pointed at her and smiled back. "You're trying to trick me!"

"Trick you?"

"That's right, you're trying to trick me into revealing the secret code. How do I know? You might be an agent of the enemy."

"Who's the enemy?"

"I don't know. Who *is* the enemy?"

"The Russians?" she suggested.

"Could be."

"How about the Germans?"

"Possible."

"Or—the South Vietnamese?"

"I thought it was the North Vietnamese?"

"One or the other."

"Yeah, well, you're the expert on enemies, but you left one out."

"Which one?"

He paused for effect. "The—Southern Californians! Ha!"

"Oh my God." She covered her face. "I'm caught."

"That's right. You can spot 'em a mile away. They come flashing up the freeway belching smoke and fire and they all look like Buicks, new Buicks."

"You mean I look like a new Buick?" She looked as if she were about to break into laughter or tears.

"Oh, no. You look like one of us."

She relaxed her dramatic disbelief. "Well, that's good. I think."

"Do you still want to know the password?"

"Sure."

"It's changeling." Changeling was a word he'd read in a science fiction story.

"Changeling?"

"Changeling."

"What does it mean?"

"I don't know. I think it means 'one who changes.' Like the password, it changes all the time."

"Oh."

"Either that, or it just means 'small change.' "

"Or somebody who works for the Muni," she countered.

"Well, yeah, except that they're *exact* change. Which is like *no* change. Anyway, I think you're safe. I don't think there are any changelings anymore."

"That's too bad."

"Yeah, too bad. Or maybe it's good, who knows? After all, we don't even know what they were. They might have been awful things, real bastards."

"No," she said. "They were like unicorns, and unicorns were always gentle."

"Gentle and horny," Frankie ventured. "And you gotta watch *that* combination."

They both laughed. When Laurel laughed, her whole face took part. Her mouth, her teeth, her eyes, her cheeks. Frankie was totally entranced by her face. The combination of parts and gestures was so new, no one had ever been put together so well before. And here she was, looking and smiling at him.

He was a little nervous, really, something like the way he felt on the morning of a game. He knew that there was nothing he could do but hope that, whatever was to happen, he didn't turn out to be the one who screwed things up. And there was no telling when the potential screw-up might come. All you could do was wait.

Pauline, who had been so quiet and indifferent since her arrival, suddenly perked up as she spied Jeremy Taylor swaggering into the store. It was well known that Pauline had the hots for J.T., as did probably half a dozen other girls, but she differed from them in her total lack of restraint in the matter. Sometimes, when he spotted her attack, J.T. would literally take off, running at full tilt down the street while she chased after him some fifteen or twenty yards behind. This time he just stopped in his tracks, preparing himself to suffer the onslaught manfully.

"Be back later," said Pauline over her shoulder as she darted out of the booth. She reached him and backed him outside, gesturing and talking all the while about something of obvious import, while J.T. raised his eyes to heaven just before they disappeared through the door. Frankie thought he was behaving unusually well, all things considered.

Laurel turned back to him. "She likes him, I think."

Frankie smiled. "Yeah, could be."

They were silent then, for a moment, and Frankie realized, with a gulp, that they were suddenly alone together. What would he do?

Laurel looked up at him and smiled.

He grinned, foolishly no doubt, but there was no way to control it.

They continued to look and smile at each other in the oppressive silence. Frankie was half afraid that someone would break into their vulnerable speechlessness, and half afraid that someone wouldn't. He would have liked to have been on his way (there was a game waiting for him down at the Prayerbook court) while he could be at least reasonably confident of a good impression. On the other hand, who in the hell would leave a girl like this to meet a bunch of sweaty basketball junkies?

Shit, there was no question about it, he was a social coward.

He braced himself to ask a question, any question. Just as he began asking her why she'd moved to the city, she began saying something else and all sense was lost in the jumble of words.

But they laughed.

"Go ahead," he said.

"Well, I was just going to say that my father is up here to open up a new sales office, and that's why we moved up from Los Angeles."

Psychic, Frankie thought, psychic.

"Who does he work for?"

"He works for G.M."

"Oh. Do you move around a lot then?"

The question seemed unnaturally important to him.

"No, not really. Sometimes."

"That's good."

"He's away a lot, but when he's home, he's home all the time." She smiled. "That's always been a big deal around our house."

"Oh."

"He's always got his stories and his new jokes and the news from all over the place. He's a hard man to get to sit still."

"Yeah."

There was silence again. Frankie could tell by her eyes that she was thinking about her father. He sounded like some kind of relative that they flew in once a month to tell them dirty jokes about Detroit.

Well, that was nice, anyway. Now what?

Maybe it was a good time to go play some basketball.

He might have made a small motion in that direction, because Laurel immediately suggested that they go outside to see what happened to Pauline. That seemed like a good idea.

She was nowhere in sight, though. Only the Lactus twins graced the sidewalk outside.

Laurel leaned close to him to whisper, "What's the matter with them?"

Frankie bent toward her face. He smelled the fragrance of her hair and felt her surprising small body lightly against his own. "They're thinking."

She laughed, still in a whisper. "What are they thinking about?"

"They're thinking about whether or not to drool."

"To drool or not to drool."

"That is the question."

"Let's move, Frankie, I don't want them to hear."

"Hear? They can't hear. They're not even *here.*"

She laughed again, but she pushed him until they were out of range.

"Are they twins?" she asked, peeking surreptitiously over her shoulder.

"No," said Frankie, "not really. Actually, one's Chinese, but they're always so stoned they got to look alike."

"Oh I see."

"Right. Chromosome damage."

"Oh, my. What a shame."

"Yes, they were brilliant once, and now look at them."

"How they've fallen."

"They've fallen all right. More than once."

"What a shame."

"Yup. What a shame."

Frankie shifted his feet and took a long look up and down the block for J.T. and Pauline. Nothing. Laurel, he noticed, did the same. Still shifting back and forth restlessly, and smiling, they looked over into the park. Not too far within that leafy glade his game was at that moment proceeding, on the small court behind the trees, in the shadow of that giant stone cross. He could almost hear the pulselike sound of the game.

"One thing you've got," she said, "is Golden Gate Park. There's really nothing like it in L.A."

"No?"

"Not really. There's Balboa Park in San Diego, and that's just an incredible thing, but it's still not Golden Gate Park. Golden Gate is one of a kind. I've always envied you this," she said, gazing at the sunny green facade which faced them from across Lincoln Way.

"Well, it's yours now, too." He smiled.

"Yes," she whispered, before smiling back and saying, "and I love it."

"Good."

It occurred to him then that he might ask her to go for a walk in the park—she seemed as if she'd be inclined to agree—but he didn't want to press his luck. Instead, he thought he'd talk, off the top of his head, about the park. Nothing dangerous about that.

"I've always kind of liked it," he began, harmlessly enough. "We've always lived close by. I don't know. When I was a kid we always used to go for walks in the park, you know? On Sundays. The Japanese Tea Garden and all that. It seemed a lot bigger and greener then, but I suppose that's natural."

He looked at her and smiled, self-consciously, but it was such a lift to see the evident interest in her eyes.

"Anyway, we used to go out on Sundays—most of the time, when I was a lot younger—just to walk around and see everything. It was such a big thing, it's hard to believe now, but I think I really looked forward to it, just going out walking in the park, just the three of us. Maybe go out rowing on Stow Lake, that was always a treat. Just the three of us, floating around out there with about two hundred other boats ramming each other and plowing into each other's oars. It was something.

"And then they'd light up the Rainbow Falls every Sunday and we'd have to get by to see that. All those colors in the water coming out of nowhere, that used to knock me out when I was younger, you know? I think

I thought it was religious or something. Anyway, I remember I was quite upset when I found out there was no real falls there at all, it was all fake, even the water was pumped there from Stow Lake and they only turned the damn lights on on Sundays, just when I happened to be there. What a shuck.

"It's okay, though, because I gradually found out that the whole park is a kind of a shuck. I mean, it's all man-made, and I don't think that's entirely *bad*, you know, but, well, it came as kind of a surprise.

"They still turn on the Rainbow Falls on Sunday. I see it every once in a while, but it still makes me kind of think about the old days, you know?"

She smiled.

"The old days." Frankie shook his head. "Jesus, I sound like some kind of corpse."

She laughed with him.

"Well, you know how it is," he said.

And she did.

"Yeah, well . . ."

He was a little embarrassed at his loose-lipped performance, but she seemed to understand. Still, it was about time he was getting going.

"Say, listen, Laurel. Speaking of the Rainbow Falls, there's a basketball court right near there and right now I'm kind of expected at a game that's going on there, if you know what I mean."

"Oh, sure," she said. "And look, here comes Pauline."

Frankie looked and saw her, striding purposefully, and alone, toward them.

"Looks like he outran her," Frankie said, and Laurel smiled.

"Hey, look," he said, "I guess I should be getting along."

"Yeah."

"But I'm awfully glad I came here first."

"I'm glad you did, too."

What a wonderful thing for her to say.

"So I guess I'll be getting over to the game."

"Okay."

Now that he was really leaving, Frankie found it almost impossible to go. "Uhm, we've got a little court over by the Prayerbook Cross. That's a great big stone monument that sits up on a God-forsaken hill and commemorates the first Mass said in California or something."

Laurel smiled and tilted her head. "Hey, Frankie, are you a Catholic?"

Frankie didn't know what to say. "Uh, yeah."

"I thought so."

"Why?"

"Because the Prayerbook Cross commemorates the Book of Common Prayer, Sir Francis Drake and his people. It's a Protestant thing."

"Oh."

She was still smiling as Pauline bore down on them. Frankie felt a little silly, a little out of it, but he didn't really mind.

He said, "Hey, Laurel, are you a Protestant?"

She smiled and said, "Yeah."

He said, "I thought so," and they both laughed heartily.

"I'd better get along."

"Okay."

"But I'll see you later, okay?"

"Okay," she said, smiling brightly. "See ya."

"Yeah. See ya."

Frankie knew his mind wouldn't be strictly on the game. Laurel Travers had commanded his attention like something bright and foreign, something he could not ignore, and something to which he could not help being drawn. She remained behind, with her cousin, back inside Lopez Market. Perhaps she was surrounded in her booth by other supplicant souls. Frankie could not quite leave her behind. The Shadow was shaken.

It was a brisk, effortless walk over to the Prayerbook court for the game. Frankie walked quickly, his hands in his pockets and his mind manufacturing images of Laurel. Her bouncing brown hair. Her smile.

He could tell by the way she had looked at him that it was true, that she'd seen something in him which he'd only hoped was there. He could tell that she was looking, that she was interested. But he just couldn't quite make himself believe it. There must have been something he'd overlooked, something rather obvious to those who know, that would invalidate the whole thing. There had to be a catch.

But what if there weren't?

It was too good to be true. Frankie felt himself tingle from the inside out. His body had gone right ahead and believed it; only his mind, like a stubborn old man, preferred to wait and see.

He decided he'd wait and see—tingling all the while.

As he approached the asphalt court, Frankie heard the familiar heartbeat of the game. It was hidden from him, behind the tall reed bushes, but the rhythm was unmistakable. It was his game. His own heartbeat fell into step, disrupting the flow of his thoughts of Laurel.

Everyone was there; they had already started. It was the same group always. Sometimes others would attempt to join: stringy, stoned hippie types up from the Haight; square-jawed collegiates; or superfly, dainty black dudes in leather coats and hats; but they were all coldly tolerated until they got the message and left. This was really a serious game.

There were only about eight of them who played—usually six or so showed up at a time. Three to a side, full court. There were no teams; it was always just a chance assignment, depending upon who arrived, and when. But the players remained the same.

They were all black but Frankie. Yet Frankie was the only one who played high school basketball. Some of the group didn't go to high school, but some did and just didn't bother to go out for the team. Whatever the reason, and it sure as hell didn't bother Frankie, he was the only one.

The absolute regulars were there when Frankie stepped through the bushes: James, Charles, "Clyde," Mel, and Number 44. No one spoke when he arrived, but there was an aura of welcome about the game which only Frankie could feel. Number 44, who was a small quiet dynamo of a kid, known only by the number on his inevitable sweatshirt, glanced at him briefly and held the ball aloft in his small deft hands. It was communication enough.

The game they played was flawless, machinelike. When Frankie entered, it was as if he'd always been there. There was no transition, just the patterned break after a basket, the pause, and then rolling smoothly back into action. They'd been playing uneven sides before, so Frankie's advent evened things up, but it made little difference to the way the game was played. The teams rolled up and down the court, with only the ball, like a metronome, keeping time.

It went on like that until late in the afternoon, when the game ended and everyone walked slowly from the court, each in his own direction, to go home. Frankie was tired, which was half the reason for his surprise when he noticed the brand-new

action

painted across the old crumbling stone of the bridge over Kennedy Drive. The red paint gleamed as Frankie walked past it, changing its aspect in the declining sunlight.

The phone rang shortly after six o'clock. It was Pauline Alee, something which confused Frankie at first, since she had never called him before.

"Hi, Pauline, how are you?"

"Oh, good, good."

"Yeah?"

"How are you, Frankie?"

"Good."

She coughed. "Well . . . I'll tell you . . . you sure made an impression today."

Frankie felt a flood of satisfaction washing away the confusion. His mind presented him with a photograph of Laurel, flashing across his consciousness like a butterfly, so difficult to hold.

"What do you mean, impression?"

"Oh, come on. What do you think I mean, huh?"

"I don't know."

"I mean on my cousin, Laurel."

"Oh, on Laurel. Oh. Well. Uh, what makes you say so?"

"Oh, let's just say I know."

"Oh."

"Quite an impression."

"What kind of impression did I make?"

"A good one, I guess. Why don't you call her up and find out for yourself?"

"Call her up?"

"Sure, I'll give you the number."

"Yeah, but, I mean, why am I supposed to be calling her up, you know? Out of nowhere."

"Why not?"

"Why not? I don't know. It's just kind of a surprise, that's all."

"Five five five, eight four oh four."

"What?"

"I said, five five five, eight four oh four."

"What's that, her number?"

Pauline sounded exasperated. "Well, what'd you think it was, her measurements?"

"Yeah, well, wait a second, will you? I'll get a pencil."

555–8404. 555–8404. 555–8404. Frankie kept repeating the number to himself as he searched the drawers for a pencil. 555–8404. He wrote the number on a piece of scrap paper and stuck it in his pocket.

"Hello, Pauline?"

"Five five five, eight four oh four."

"Yeah, I got it. Okay. So maybe I'll give her a call, as soon as I think of something to say."

Pauline laughed. "Oho, you'll think of something to say, Frankie. You'll think of something."

Her voice made him retreat. There was a discomforting inflection in it, even through the telephone, which reminded him of some early embarrassment. It was such a silly connection, yet he couldn't help blushing slightly and wishing that, whatever his feeling for Laurel might be, it might have remained something privately his, and not discussed over chuckling telephone lines in teenage whispers through the neighborhood. It was as if it had already lost something.

"Okay, Pauline, we'll see."

"Okay, Frankie, talk to you later."

"Yeah, bye-bye."

"'Bye."

Frankie was numb as he hung up. Visions of Laurel and nightmares of Pauline vied in his consciousness for control. Slowly, but decisively, Laurel's promised joy won out.

He was almost smiling as he walked into the living room. His mother and father, having finished dinner, were watching something on TV. His father was settled in his favorite spot, an old patchwork easy chair located just across the room from the television. He was not drunk, not entirely. Instead he was passing through that loose, soppy stage between one drunk and the next. He was talkative, relaxed, pliable as warm rubber in his shallow, temporary glory.

"Looka that foolishness, will you?" He pointed vaguely toward the television. His mother, who was drinking coffee and smoking, turned and watched. It was a documentary on weirdoes or something.

"They all got pigtails, for Chrissake."

His mother watched, her eyes blinking from time to time.

The announcer told them that there were approximately 40,000 Hare Krishna followers in the U.S. and that their number was growing every day. The picture showed a circle of saffron-robed, sexless people dancing and chanting around a statue of a pissing cherub in some Chicago park. They were all male, or so it seemed to Frankie, and he wondered what happened to the girls. Or maybe some of them were girls, it was hard to tell.

"Looka that foolishness, will you?" his father repeated.

"Oh, come on, Frank," his mother said, out of the tired side of her mouth.

"Yeah, but hell, those kids gotta be crazy to do that, you know? It just doesn't make sense to me."

It didn't make sense to Frankie, either, but he felt obligated to say something. "Well, different strokes for different folks."

"Huh?"

"To each his own."

"Oh, yeah, to each his own, but gee, it just doesn't make any sense to me."

Frankie looked at his mother and she returned his glance. She shrugged her shoulders and took another sip from her coffee.

The announcer went on to describe shots of various Hindus, and of octopus-armed statues and the like. Then back to the Hare Krishna house in Chicago, where the initiates were gathered around a nervous bowl of rice.

His father smiled and said, "Good luck." His head sank back against the chair and his eyelids descended gradually, like an electric elevator's last trip to the bottom floor.

Frankie and his mother watched the rest of the program in silence. She finished her coffee and smoked another cigarette. She blinked lazily as the television image played its cold gaze against her eyes.

Frankie got up during the last commercial and moved out to the phone. He fully intended to dial 555–8404, although he wasn't at all sure what he was going to say. Something like "Hey, I just got finished watching a show on weirdoes and I thought of you."

Probably not that, but something.

Anyway, it was academic, since the phone rang at his end before he could reach it to make his call. Intuition told him it might even be Laurel. But it wasn't, it was Jeremy Taylor.

"Hey, Frankie, I gotta talk to you."

"What's the matter?"

"I don't want to talk about it now. Can you meet me at Lopez in about fifteen minutes?"

"Sure. I guess so."

"Okay, see you then." And he hung up.

When Frankie walked into a sleepy Lopez Market, J.T. was already there, pacing back and forth next to a booth. He grabbed Frankie and sat him down at the booth. Two coffees were already there and steaming.

"Look, Frankie, we gotta do something."

"What do you mean?" Frankie sipped his coffee.

"Well, I mean, it's silly, you know? All we do is hang around here and take a lot of shit from everyone and it's just a waste of time."

Frankie nodded. Old J.T. was really excited about something. Frankie wondered if he'd finally been shot down by some girl. What a crash. His flashing turquoise eyes, those slayers of female hearts, were running absentmindedly about the room, only bumping suddenly into Frankie when he spoke. "Do you know what I mean?"

"Okay. So what do you want to do?"

"*Some*thing. Something half decent for a change."

Frankie shrugged his shoulders. "Okay, okay. Join the Salvation Army."

"Come on, Frankie, I'm being serious." He looked serious. "No shit, really."

Frankie shrugged his shoulders again.

J.T. became conspiratorial, leaning across the table. "Listen, I got it all figured out. I figured I'd ask you because you're the one person I could think of who'd understand what I'm talking about."

Frankie accepted the compliment warily.

"Okay." J.T. lowered his hands, palms down, to the table. "This is the plan. We gotta get out of here, right?"

"Right."

"We gotta do something, right?"

"Right."

"Something worthwhile."

"Right."

"And we gotta do it now."

"Right." All these "rights" were getting to Frankie, but he thought, for the sake of the argument, that he'd agree. What was the harm?

"Because we just can't put up with all this bullshit any longer."

"Right."

"We've gotta move away, get into something else, and move away as soon as we can."

Hold it. "Wait a minute, J.T. How about letting me in on what exactly it is that you're talking about?"

"Well, this is it. Let's split tonight for Portland, Oregon."

"Portland, Oregon?"

"Yeah, they got some kind of Jesuit Provincial up there, they'll take us in, and we can study to be Jesuits."

"J.T., you have got to be shitting me."

"No, I'm serious, I'm serious."

"Yeah, but running away to a seminary? You've got to be kidding!"

"I'm not. I'm serious. We could do it."

"Wow."

"What's wrong with that?"

Frankie shook his head. J.T. looked surprised. He raised his hands, palms out. "Frankie, why not? I mean, we don't have to stay if we don't like it, you know?"

Frankie shook his head.

"Look, Frankie, what's wrong here?" Down went his hands, with a crash, to the table. "I thought you'd go for this. It's a big chance to break out of here. You were always a little on the wild side; I thought you'd appreciate this."

"J.T., wait a second. Look. I'd be willing to go along with you, sure. But I've got to at least want to a *little* bit, you know?"

J.T. was silent, sulking. His plan was temporarily sabotaged. Frankie watched him. He felt just slightly guilty for refusing the invitation, even though he realized that this was just some emotional fling on J.T.'s part. Something to get back at his father, no doubt.

"What's the problem, J.T., your old man again?"

J.T. snapped his reply through his teeth. "That asshole?"

Okay, that was it all right. There was nothing further to say.

On the way home he tried to imagine the change to his life which might have occurred had he taken J.T. up on his proposition. Father O'Day—it sounded as if it were straight out of some grade B delinquency flick. His life story, played by Bing Crosby. Or Mick Jagger.

It was, of course, idle speculation, since there was no imaginable way that either he or J.T. could ever have made it that far. It was probably the most ridiculous suggestion he had ever heard. Which did nothing at all to explain why he felt so unsure of himself, and so wistful, about turning it down.

He didn't call Laurel that night, but he did see her the next day at Lopez. The Lactus twins were on the sidewalk when he arrived. Like flotsam and jetsam, they sat staring straight ahead, with jaws resting unnaturally on their chests. He stepped over their listless, out-stretched legs and entered the store.

There were ten or fifteen people in the store, but Frankie recognized Laurel's presence at once, not with his eyes, but with a curdling, anticipatory knowledge in his stomach. And she *was* there. He saw her head then, from behind, in a booth with Pauline. He was poised to rush to her when he noticed that she was talking to— who else would it be?

J.T.

Apparently, J.T. had recovered from his attack of whooping vocation of the night before and decided to return to the land of the (barely) living. And Laurel was clearly the most living thing around.

Frankie held back then, with a temporary weak-ness in his arms, and bought a peanut cluster at the counter. He was biting it, and hearing the disembodied *crunch crunch* in his head, when he noticed Pauline leaning over toward Laurel. He knew what she must be saying.

She didn't turn. He waited, but her head remained fixed to the front.

He didn't have any choice, then. He went to the booth.

"Hi."

"Hi." Pauline smiled before he'd actually arrived.

Laurel looked up, smiling her wide, wonderful smile. Frankie watched the pupils of her eyes, to see if he could detect a dilation or enlargement as she looked at him. He'd heard that such a reaction was a natural biological response to viewing something a person found attractive. Her pupils were unchanged, though, as far as he could tell. He didn't know whether to doubt himself or the natural biological response.

"Well," he said, "how are you doing?"

Everyone was fine. J.T. said good-bye; he had to leave. He smiled at everyone, particularly the new girl, and left. He might have been thinking of his religious experience of the night before and, no doubt, had decided that more solitude was necessary. Or else he was reluctant to have Frankie bring up the subject of his vocation in front of the others. Not that he would have.

In any event, he was gone, which suited Frankie well enough.

Laurel and he took very little time to get back together. She slid in toward the wall and invited him to sit down, which he did with no hesitation. Their talk went from their memories of yesterday to the smiling silences that were so new to today. How difficult it was to hold his nervous eyes on hers. And how exciting when he did, even for a moment, and saw her own eyes looking back.

Pauline excused herself, in that manic way of hers, and left them alone. Laurel looked up at him and smiled. "Hey, nice seeing you again."

Frankie felt washed with warmth. "Yeah, you, too."

"No basketball today?"

"Oh"—he shrugged—"a little later, I guess. There's time."

Her smile agreed that there was all the time they'd need.

"What about you? What are you doing later on?"

"I don't know. Going over to Pauline's, I suppose."

"Pauline's, huh?"

"Yeah."

"What about tonight?"

She smiled, as if from relief, he thought. "Nothing. Staying home."

"Do you have to?"

"Well, I don't know. What are you suggesting?"

"I guess I'm suggesting that you come out."

"Where?"

"Anywhere. I'll meet you there."

"You'll meet me—anywhere?"

"Well, you know, here, or someplace else if you want."

Laurel smiled and turned away from him suddenly. She stared for a moment into the empty booth across from them. When she turned back it was clear that she had reached some sort of decision.

"Okay."

"Great. Where should I meet you? Here?"

"No. You'll have to come by and get me."

"To *your* house?"

"Yes. My father is very weird about these things, you know what I mean? Particularly since we just moved here."

"You mean he'll want to meet me?"

"Right. And we'll have to tell him we're going to the movies."

"The movies?"

"Oh, well, you know. He's really one of those old-fashioned type people who always feel that people have to be 'going' somewhere if they're going out."

"Oh."

"You should meet him anyway, he's okay. I think you'll like him." She smiled.

Frankie couldn't help smiling back. "Sure I will."

So it was settled then, they were going to the movies. What movie they were going to see, where Frankie was going to get the money, how and when they were to be transported there, all these questions remained unanswered, but he didn't care in the least.

Laurel seemed to sense something of his train of thought. She put her hand on his arm and looked up at him with her eyebrows raised and her face so softly concerned. "We don't really have to go, you know, if you really don't want to. We just have to say we are."

"We don't?"

"Not if you don't want to."

Frankie didn't know whether he wanted to or not, by that time. He was still too dizzy from his trying to keep up with this quick exciting girl to have any opinions whatever about anything. He did finally manage to decide that the movies weren't an absolute necessity for him to live through the evening, and his expression must have conveyed this to Laurel.

"Okay." She smiled. "I didn't really want to go that much, either."

"No?"

"Nah. But don't forget to say we're going or you'll blow the whole thing."

"I won't forget."

"Good." Her face relaxed.

Frankie shivered in his seat. He couldn't even wait.

"What time are you coming?"

"I don't know. What do you think?"

"How about seven-thirty?"

"Okay. Seven-thirty it is."

"Good."

They both nodded, reflections of each other, in the slow, quiet booth.

Frankie cleared his throat and asked, "What should I wear?"

"What?"

"I mean, should I wear anything special?"

Laurel smiled and shook her head with amusement. Frankie felt like some lovable hick who'd just asked if he could piss in the street.

"Whatever you want," she said. "Whatever you think you should wear."

"Okay."

"Good."

It was time to go. Frankie repeated his instructions for her, just to make sure, as he slid from the booth to the aisle. He made his departure in a clumsy (but lovable) exchange of waves and good-byes. He was almost to the door when he called back, as unobtrusively as he could, "Hey, Laurel, what movie are we going to see, anyway?"

"How about . . . *The Great Gatsby*?"

"The one with Robert Redford? Is that still around?"

"It's part of a Redford Film Festival, down at the Esquire. Did you see it when it first came out?"

"Nope."

"Oh well, I guess you'll miss it again tonight."

"I guess I will."

"Okay. Seven-thirty. See ya."

"See ya."

He was still looking over his shoulder at Laurel as he backed out of the store and stepped directly into Billy Lyons.

"Frankie. Whatcha doing?"

"Billy. Nothing."

Frankie continued to feel clumsy. It was something he would have to get over. Billy motioned him off to the side of the store; he had something to tell him.

"Frankie," he whispered, smacking his gum around inside his mouth and glancing sharply from side to side. "Something big."

"What is it?"

Billy Lyons was the original speed freak, except that he didn't use speed. If he had ever tried it, he would probably have fallen asleep. Drugs worked that way sometimes. But Billy didn't need any drug. He'd managed to acquire his bony, dancing body, his dark sunken eyes, and his crazy nervous paranoia directly from nature. How lucky can you get, huh? Frankie couldn't picture his surviving past thirty-five. It was either a heart attack or a straightjacket or a job in the prison laundry, where he'd probably drive everyone nuts with his maniac escape attempts, none of which would ever be even remotely successful.

"Can't tell you yet. Gotta talk to my brother first."

"Okay."

His brother was a strange character. He must have been about thirty, tall, tattooed, skinny like Billy, and strictly from *The Blackboard Jungle.* Slicked-back hair, cigarette dangling grimly from his leathery lips, he never said much but there was evidence of a constant inner turmoil going on somewhere behind those thin dark eyes. He was tough, or he must have been, since no one was ever foolish enough to find out for sure.

"Soon, though," Billy assured him. "Maybe next week. I don't know. I gotta talk to my brother."

Frankie nodded.

Billy just shook his head and broke out laughing. "Frankie, you're just not going to believe this, you're not going to believe it."

"What?"

"I can't tell you yet."

He was still laughing and clapping his hands as he

disappeared into Lopez. Frankie went off to lose himself in the Prayerbook basketball game.

It was love, of course, that much was certain. Frankie had never been in love before, not really. He'd thought he was, perhaps, but he guessed in retrospect that it was infatuation, not love. He'd had some powerful infatuations, but never the total immersion which he felt when he was with Laurel. And never did he have such hope that his desire might be so honestly returned. His earlier attempts at love had been mostly stillborn, or misdirected, or just inept. He'd believed himself in love with Ophelia Jacobs during the whole of his first two years of high school. Being in love with Ophelia was like being in love with a pan of water. It was there all right, but there wasn't much you could do with it. Ophelia must have known that he was attracted to her, and she never did anything to dissuade him, but she never did anything to encourage him, either. She never did *anything.* He'd wondered if she'd simply preferred it that way, *nolo contendere*, and he guessed that she had. What was a bit more difficult for him to apprehend was his own protracted devotion to an end which would probably never be attained.

The whole thing was an emotional waste of time, but perhaps that was what he had wanted. "In pursuit of the unattainable"—it had such a romantic ring to it. Since he never mentioned the nature of his pursuit to anyone else, he lost no face, and his marathon of attachment eventually dwindled off into a mild remembrance. The race was over, called because of darkness.

Frankie was no saint, though, no Sir Galahad on a single-minded and chaste trail to the Castle Virginal. Not by a long shot. He'd lost his virginity early, to a very fast Dutch girl named Fay Sirke Vouldray. Fay was the original basketball groupie; she balled entire teams during halftime. Coaches went crazy as they attempted their inane pep talks and players kept disappearing, soon to return, slightly flushed but infinitely more relaxed. She could change the course of an entire season, taking a young and nervous team and sending them back out onto the court with a renewed vigor and a steely confidence which the opposition found difficult to match. She got to Frankie on a number of occasions, knocking him off like one of those weighted dolls on a carnival pitch-stand, before moving on to her next assignment.

Frankie had fallen in love with her, too, believe it or not. Of course it was hopeless, but Frankie spent a few weeks in misery before his body finally relented and he could again watch her jacking off the backcourt without wanting to kill himself.

He should have known: She wasn't a person, someone to fall in love with; she was a legend, an idea. They said she would do anything, anything. Much as he wanted to, Frankie never really got to know her before she disappeared. Legend had it (and it was not at all improbable) that she succumbed to a chill while standing in the rain for seven days and nights under a tree across from Rick Barry's house waiting for him to return home. The cruel legend further stated that the house of her vigil was one which Barry had vacated for larger quarters a year earlier. So she died for nought, for whatever that's worth.

Other than Fay, there had been one or two other sexual connections, but nothing really memorable. And nothing really close to being in love. Not until Laurel. How could he possibly believe it?

Which explained his nervousness as he reached for her doorbell, lighted like a tiny candle in the purple twilight. When he touched it, it seemed warm, as if to presage the life which moved mysteriously about inside the house. He inspected his reflection in the window and decided he looked neat enough. Her father answered the door.

"Come in, come in." He was smiling hospitably, and being very officious.

The house was rather new and carpeted and very typical of the section in which she lived. Their color television was on in the corner of the soft sunken living room, and Laurel's older brother interrupted his watching long enough to check out his sister's date. He was satisfied, apparently, and gave Frankie a manly nod, with a hint of amusement in his smile. Her brother looked like a football player, bullet-headed and not exceptionally intelligent. Frankie found himself wondering if it was hereditary.

"Laurel," her father announced, "your date is here."

Frankie heard her say that she'd be right down. This prompted her father to offer Frankie a seat, which he accepted, having no idea whatsoever how to go about refusing it.

"So"—her father rubbed his hands and sat across from Frankie—"where you going?"

Right off, the interrogation. "We're going to the movies, I guess."

He shook his crew-cut head, up and down, thoughtfully, with his hands clasped in front of him. His hair was red, going to gray, but it must have been flashing red in his youth, if he'd ever let enough of it grow. He was a short, stocky man, built like a fireplug they sometimes say, but a lot of his stock had gone to fat and it hung over his belt like a mass of whipped cream overflowing a dish.

"June!" he yelled suddenly, over his shoulder.

A thin, stringy, but not unattractive woman appeared. Mrs. Travers, certainly.

"See if the boy wants anything, will you?"

"Oh, nothing, thanks."

"Sure?"

"Oh, yes. I'm fine, thanks."

"Okay."

After playing with his fingers for a while, Laurel's father exploded into another question. "Have you met Carl here?"

Frankie turned obligingly and said hello. Carl smiled his familiar smile and offered Frankie the handful of popcorn he was holding.

"Oh, no, thanks."

"Carl's going to Stanford, you know."

Stanford? God, the school must be going to the dogs.

"Gonna play some football."

"Oh, yeah?" Frankie tried to be polite. He turned toward Carl. "What position do you play?"

Carl didn't answer—his mouth was full of popcorn and his eyes were glued to the television, where a runaway horse was pulling a stuntman through a mile of cactus.

His father said, "Quarterback."

Good God, the school *was* going to the dogs. How did they expect him to remember the plays?

His father got up then and leaned over to rub his son's head. "Gonna be the next Fran Tarkenton."

Frankie tried to look impressed. Carl pulled his head away from his father's hand. "Dad, come on, not while I'm eatin' popcorn."

"Okay, okay." He sat back down. "So, tell me, Frankie, what movie you going to see tonight?"

"The Great Gatsby."

"Oh yeah, right. Hemingway, wasn't it?"

"I guess so." No sense riling him.

"Yes, yes. They made that movie a bunch of times already. Alan Ladd was in it, if memory serves."

Frankie nodded a polite agreement.

"Yeah, and Joan Fontaine or someone, too."

Sure thing.

His face twisted into a configuration which suggested deep thought, or sudden enlightenment, until it was relieved by a shouting, again, over his shoulder, "June!"

"Yes," she said, when she appeared, carrying a wet pot, through the kitchen door.

"I thought Laurel already saw *The Great Gatsby,* didn't she?"

"Why, I don't think so. Ask her."

"Laurel!"

Her voice said that she was almost ready.

He shook his head. "That girl, I don't know. She's always putting something on. Never on time."

Frankie smiled, politely he hoped.

At last Laurel appeared. She wore jeans and a lightly starched shirt and carried her jacket. Frankie, who had worn the neatest things he had, still felt under-dressed. No one else seemed to notice.

Her father rose and greeted her, "Well, well, here she is, here she is. Ready at last."

She smiled back at him, like a little girl, Frankie thought, and allowed her father to help her on with her jacket. Only then was she brought over to Frankie, like a small, precious gift with which, against someone's better judgment, he was to be temporarily entrusted. Frankie's mouth was dry; he licked his lips and immediately regretted it. He must have looked like a pervert, salivating and palpitating all over the room like a runaway gob of grease. But no one mentioned it.

"All right now," said her father, "here she is, you take good care of my little girl and have a good time at the movies."

"Thanks, Daddy."

"What time'll you be home?"

"About eleven, eleven-thirty, twelve." She smiled at him, out of habit.

"Eleven-thirty."

"Oh, Daddy, we'll try."

She turned then toward Frankie. Her arm slipped

into his and they left the house. The warm breath of the
ocean in the outside air teased out his spirits from where
they'd been hiding, and he was remarkably sure that
this night would be a special one indeed.

After a Coke and some preliminary conversation at
Lopez, they went out by themselves and walked in the
fragrant starry evening. Heading vaguely toward the
beach, they walked slowly and a bit awkwardly, bumping into each other at times and smiling. It was very
relaxed and timeless.

Frankie learned, along the way, something of Laurel's background, of her family. They'd come from
L.A., and before that from Corpus Christi, Texas,
where her father had been working his way up through
the ranks of the automobile company. Although she
never mentioned it, Frankie got the impression that
they were now rather well off. He also came to know
that she absolutely idolized her father, a sentiment
which escaped him entirely.

They had a boat, which they kept somewhere
between San Francisco and L.A., and plenty of cars,
and their house, and also a summer place up at Lake
Tahoe. It was this last which had the most ominous
import.

"You go up there every summer?"

"Yup. Every summer."

"For the whole summer?"

"Yup. We do. Even Daddy does, really. He stays
in town during the week and comes up first thing Saturday morning."

"Oh yeah?"

"Yup. He loves it up there. It's so fresh, you know?"

"Oh, definitely. I like it, too." A small lie; Frankie had never been there.

"The water's so cool and clean, it feels like it was just scrubbed and poured into the lake."

"Yeah." Frankie hoped that his concern was apparent to her. "When do you go up?"

"Usually in July and August."

"Oh."

They were quiet then, thinking. There was no way he could think of to ask the question, but he felt sure that Laurel was preoccupied with the same thing he was, her vacation. It was so close.

As their silence continued, it buoyed him up, made him tender, and hopeful.

"Come with me," he said at last. "Let's forget the beach. I want to show you something."

Her thoughtful eyes smiled back. Okay.

They hopped the short stone wall and set off into the park. Frankie led her over a trail strewn with pine needles. It rose gently up the side of a soft dark hillock, thick with trees. When they reached the top, Frankie indicated that she should sit down, which she did, leaning back comfortably against an old pine. Frankie joined her.

"It's nice here, isn't it?"

"Yeah," she agreed.

And it was. The trees kept them sheltered and private while, below them, hysterical cars rushed past on the divided road, or groups of people strode noisily by on the sidewalk. It was nice.

She looked up at the grove of evergreens around her. "Only in Golden Gate Park," she said.

Frankie leaned over and kissed her, on her round flushed lips. She kissed him back and they were both smiling when they parted. Frankie was almost laughing. "Well, what about this place, huh?"

She smiled. "It's pretty."

He leaned his head back. "It's good to be alone here and relax like this every once in a while."

"Yup, it is."

"Someplace to think, or just let loose some excess fatigue, you know?"

"Yeah."

"It's kind of a feeling of power, divorced from the world at last and just observing it." He swept his arm in an arc along the path of the lighted street, dismissing it with a gesture. " 'Cast a cold eye On life, on death. Horseman, pass by!' "

Laurel waited, and spoke. "I know. Was that a poem?"

"Right. William Butler Yeats."

"Oh." She paused, then said, "Frankie, you know you're really an unusual person, do you know that?"

"Unusual?" He laughed self-consciously.

"No, I mean out of the ordinary, extraordinary, really." She was being most serious in her voice.

"Oh, I don't know."

"You are."

"Yeah, well . . ."

"Do you write?"

"What?"

"Do you write things yourself? You know, poems, stories?"

Frankie actually hesitated. He thought of saying something about his walls, about his silly minor notoriety, but he couldn't. He just didn't know how to begin.

"No, not really."

"You ought to try it."

"Yeah, well . . ."

" 'Cause you're really a lot more sensitive than most of the other boys I've known, really."

What other boys? he thought.

"You ought to try it," she said.

"Someday."

"I think you'd be good at it."

Laurel was definitely a person worth talking to. She made him feel like some brave and talented explorer, swollen with worth and confidence, standing on the shores of his next adventure. The whole world was at his feet. Still, it was time to change the subject.

He pointed out at the vista before them and asked, "Well, how do you like *The Great Gatsby*?"

"Great. Really lavish."

"Cast of thousands, huh?"

"You bet. Hey, there's Gatsby over there getting ready to throw a party in that gas station."

"Oh yeah?"

"Yeah. And there's Mia Farrow trying to hitch a ride back to her place. She's just wearing that army jacket disguise over her flashy sequined gown to throw the party crashers off."

"Is that it?"

"That's it."

"Quite a movie. Hey, Laurel, in case anyone ever asks, what was the movie about, anyway? I mean, I don't want to come across like a *total* dummy, you know?"

She laughed. "They might think you slept right through it."

"Right. Who knows?"

"Okay. Ah, what do you want to know?"

"Well, just what the movie was about, in case anyone asks."

"Hmm. Well. It's about this rich flamboyant bachelor named Gatsby who falls in love with the beautiful Daisy Buchanan. And she falls in love with him, too. She is, however, married, and that puts a crimp on things as far as Gatsby is concerned. He throws giant parties every weekend and people come from all over to go to them, without even knowing who he *is*, you understand. He doesn't care. All he wants is Daisy.

"Well, Daisy and he become lovers all right. You see, they used to know each other a long time ago, but it didn't work out. All this time, Gatsby's been waiting to meet her again, and finally he does. He's been all around the world, he went from poor to rich, but the important thing to him is Daisy. And when he meets her, well, she finds that she loves him, too.

"Now, Daisy's husband, Tom, doesn't have to know about Gatsby but Gatsby tells him, just to bring it out in the open. The impression I got was that it could have continued on the sly, but out in the open—no way.

"Anyway, Daisy can't take it and she runs away, driving Gatsby's car over some poor woman in the process, but . . . well . . . the final thing is that she stays with Tom, her idiot husband, instead of going with Gatsby. Daisy is a real jerk here, of course. No one in her right mind would have passed up Gatsby for Tom."

"No one?"

"No one. *I* would have jumped for Gatsby in a minute."

Frankie broke out laughing. "You *would*?"

Laurel blushed, detectable even in the darkness. "Well, sure, in the context of the movie, of course. Tom was just so—stupid, and Gatsby was so—exotic and handsome."

"Well, why didn't Daisy go with Gatsby then?"

"Oh, I don't know. It was almost like she went into a trance. She just stayed with Tom out of habit or something, as if she couldn't really take the chance of breaking out of her routine. I don't know, it was strange."

"Didn't you say she was in love with Gatsby?"

"Yeah, she was."

"Well, then, why . . . ?"

"I don't know, Frankie," she interrupted. "I can't explain it. She just couldn't do it, I guess."

"So what did Gatsby do?"

"He didn't do anything. He just kind of moped around a lot, hid in her bushes and things like that."

"Oh."

"Well, anyway," Laurel continued with the plot, "the person whose wife was run over by Gatsby's car, Mr. Wilson, he comes around and shoots him in the pool."

"Shoots who?"

"Gatsby. It's really sad, believe me. He really gets the old shaft all right. And all for being so rich and handsome and desirable."

"Sounds a little unnatural to me."

"Well, you had to be there, you had to be there."

"Oh, I see." Frankie put his arm around her shoulders and drew her close. "Hey, if this movie's so good, how about being quiet so I can catch the end of it?"

He kissed her again. It seemed so much more natural than the first time, as if they'd been doing it for years. Laurel came to meet him and his shoulders tingled with the pressure of her arms, new and gentle and active to her fingertips, softly ruffling the loose hair at the nape of his neck. It was a long and wet and comfortable kiss. When they eased off, he was unwilling to allow his lips to leave her face. They stayed at her cheek, touching the side of her mouth, then down to her jaw and up to the wispy hair that rose and fell in transparent rushes next to her ear.

Her eyes, which had been closed, opened slowly and looked up at him as he leaned back from her face. They flashed momentarily in the darkness, so alive and unexpected that he broke into a smile. He couldn't help squeezing her tighter, even laughing out loud with happiness. Laurel smiled and he rocked her in his arms.

As they got to know each other better, as they got

to know the rhythms of each other's bodies, they relaxed and lent themselves more surely to each other. Frankie could have kissed her until he died. With his arms around her, he felt the strange soft pressure of her breast against his forearm. He moved his arm only slightly, neither tempting nor abandoning fate.

It was during their most passionate kiss that he felt her hand on his leg, just above the knee. It felt so comforting, so tender there. She caressed him as they kissed and Frankie squeezed his forearm against her, compressing her breast. Her hand kept moving on his leg, at first soothing and then tantalizing him. He could feel her fingers through his pants as they moved in an impetuous massage over his tingling skin. Her hand began to move up then, more quickly than he would have imagined, directly to the top. She grasped him through his pants and held to him tightly, substituting pressure for movement of her hand.

The strange thing was that Frankie was even more surprised than excited. It was just that no one had ever done that to him before, *no one.* Not even Fay. No one had ever touched him like that, so quick and certain and confident in every way. It was entirely different from just sexual excitement, it was beyond that. It was like an invasion.

It took him a while to come down from the shock of the experience, but he did, and the recovery was smooth and enjoyable in the extreme. Her hand squeezed and caressed and he could feel her outlining him with her fingers. He expected her to go further but she didn't. After a while, he slipped back into his physical passion and kissed her unreservedly, all over her face and lips. His hands emulated the daring which hers had shown him as they rushed madly all over her body, touching a thousand new and wonderful places that were hers, that were Laurel, all over. She not only let him do it, she even sighed, so deeply, through her kiss. This is making love, he thought, this is what making love is all about.

They went on like that for a while, kissing and touching each other wildly and heedlessly, breathing heavily, hearing the frenzied rush of the warm blood through their heads, before they retired at last to rest in each other's arms.

Little was said between them after that; they had done their talking earlier. When they parted at Laurel's house, they were truly lovers, and the kiss they shared then might have been one for which they had prepared forever.

Frankie had trouble getting to sleep that night. He kept thinking about her small, eager, girlish hand, grasping his swelling penis through his pants. He tried to change the subject, but it seemed to be the only scene his mind would play. He even masturbated, thinking that would do the trick, but to no avail. Finally, he tossed and turned for an indeterminate time before passing over the brink to sleep.

Frankie and Laurel met at their special place whenever they could. She couldn't get out every night, but she usually managed a night on the weekends and sometimes a night during the week. Every Wednesday night was their movie night; that much was settled. Frankie had to put in his appearance at the house, listen to her father make various pronouncements concerning the state of the world, share a bowl of popcorn with her brother, that sort of thing, but he survived.

When they reached the park, and their own hill, they set upon each other like starving children, ravenous in their kisses and embraces. As soon as they lay back on their mat of pine needles, Frankie felt Laurel's strong foreign hand run all over his body, coming at last to the places which were so warm and so unused to a girl's attention. He'd never gotten over the feeling he experienced then.

He explored and caressed her with equal vitality, touching and massaging everything within reach. Firmly and carefully he rubbed the seam of her jeans between her legs and felt the material grow warm and wet as she reacted. And she sighed. She squeezed him until he was on the verge of exploding, and he moaned at her through their kiss. It was absurd, they couldn't keep it up, they had to go somewhere. But they didn't.

Once or twice, during his wild rubbing and caressing, Frankie tried to unzip the fly of her jeans. Whatever it was that she did, and he couldn't be sure, it was some movement which told him, no, don't. And he obeyed. He could reach over at her waist and down to feel the soft silk of her underwear, or the miraculous nascent hair beneath it, but he couldn't go beyond that. He could feel and caress her through her pants, but not inside, at least not with her fly down. Those were the rules. They never talked about it, but it was understood.

They talked about everything else, though: basketball (her knowledge surprised him), politics, food (that was mostly her subject; Frankie didn't know that much about food, although he was willing to learn), drink (Frankie's subject; he could tell he impressed her with his precocious exploits in teenage debauchery), even love.

He'd asked her once, point-blank, in the midst of a very passionate moment, if she loved him.

She hesitated, and looked down toward their legs, side by side on the soft ground.

"Whaddya think?" he prompted her.

"I'm thinking."

It must be close, he thought, and he wondered at his nerve in even asking such a question. It had seemed so natural when it came out. As he thought about it, he found he was suddenly pleased that he had ventured to ask the question. It was good that he had done it.

She looked back up at him and saw his smile. She gave him hers in return. "How can you ask me such a thing?"

"It was easy."

"Oh, sure, it was easy for you. What about me? It's not so easy for me to come up with the answer."

"Well, you don't have to . . ."

"How about you, Frankie?" she whispered. "Do you love me?"

"I asked you first," he said and smiled.

She moved her hand to his and ran her fingers gently across the tops of his knuckles, "Oh, Frankie."

Her mood was so very very serious that Frankie could make no reply. He sat and waited.

"Frankie, it's so early."

His voice, when it came, was a whisper like hers. "I know."

"Give us some time."

"I know."

"We'll find out." She smiled as if she were about to cry. "We'll find out soon enough."

He smiled back. "I know."

They squeezed each other then, in that soft moment, and smiled. Frankie believed firmly, and irrefutably, that she loved him.

It was a short scene he would always remember.

On the other hand, it was also on a Wednesday movie night, in the park, that they had their first argument. It was ever so small, really, and it was about—of all things—money.

It started when Laurel said she couldn't see why people based their whole lives on the Almighty Dollar, why they spent all their time striving and grasping for money, while they allowed the rest of their lives to slip away from them like water through their tired, bony hands.

The whole thing snuck up on Frankie. There was no reason why the statement should have threatened him so. Yet he couldn't help finding himself suddenly in the position of defender for all those millions whose lives are so cavalierly dismissed by such a statement.

"Laurel, not everyone is a John D. Rockefeller, for Christ's sake."

"I'm not talking about John D. Rockefeller. I'm talking about the ones who turn their lives into a drudgery of money, you know? Like that's all they can do to hold themselves together."

"Maybe they *have* to hold themselves together, did you ever think of that? Maybe they *have* to do that."

She shook her head. "I'm not talking about the poor, either. I'm talking about the middle-class types who think nothing of their families, their children, their wives, anything but their money. Every day, more money, not more love, not more enjoyment in their lives—more money."

"Yeah, well, I guess there are people like that, but I don't see how you can condemn everybody who works to make things a little better for themselves and their families just because it takes money to do it."

"It's not that, Frankie, it's just the money, itself. Money doesn't *mean* anything, you know? It's just a possession, it's just something that happens to you, that's all."

"Sure. It happens to you if you're rich."

"But being rich isn't everything, don't you see that?"

"I see it. I see it. But I just don't understand it. What does rich mean, anyway? A thousand? A million? Ten million?"

"Being rich means having more money than you can use. Having more money than you can enjoy, you know? Having more money than makes your life enjoyable."

"But how can you say that?"

"I can say it because it's true."

"But how can you say how much money makes your life enjoyable? How do you know?"

"Frankie. It's obvious. It's obvious how much you can use and how much you can't. It's right up front. It's only the addiction to money that makes you go on."

Frankie shook his head. The whole argument smacked of unreality. What was real? It certainly wasn't judgments like the ones they were making.

He felt pent up, constrained, as if there were something inside him, some magic germane fact, that was boiling and ready to explode, but he just couldn't locate it.

"Laurel, there's just more to it than that. Can't you see it?"

"No there isn't, Frankie, no there isn't. It's as simple as that, and the problem is that everyone wants to make it more complicated."

"But it *is* complicated, goddamit, it's more complicated than a stupid little judgment that money is the root of all evil."

"I never said that. And it's not a 'stupid little judgment' at all."

Now Laurel seemed to be getting angry. He looked at her and it dawned on him that what he was arguing against was not her statements so much as her making them. It wasn't what she said (he half agreed with that), but it was something about her advancing them as her position which rankled him.

"Laurel, this is a stupid discussion."

"No, it's not stupid."

"It's pointless."

"No, it's not. It's important, it could be the main problem in the world today. No one knows what to do with the world's wealth, how to divide it up. No one knows how much of a share each person needs. . . ."

"Well, then, how in hell would you know?"

"I'd . . ."

"How in hell would you know how people who've never had any money, any power, would feel? You've always had it. You've always had it given to you."

"That's not true."

"Whatever you wanted, you could always buy it."

"That's not true."

"Of course it is. You don't know what it's like to be deprived, to have something you know you can't afford, someplace you know you'll never get to, some things you know you'll have to work your ass off for, like just your basic necessities, food and a roof over your head and heat—you never had to worry about those things."

"I had to worry, Frankie. I don't know if you think we were always rich or something, but it just isn't true. We had to work very hard for everything. We never had a house until I was six years old; we lived in apartments. I never got everything I wanted; I had to work for it."

"Sure."

"I did. I baby-sat for any extra money I needed. I get a ten-dollar allowance every week and I have to account for every penny of it, every Sunday. I bring my book to my father and I account for every penny of the previous week's allowance. Only then do I get my next week's allowance. I don't know what you think about me, but it isn't true. I never had it easy; my father taught me very early the value of money, because we never had any when I was young, we had to earn it. My father had to work his way up from the bottom."

"And that's what made him such a good father?"

"No."

"Scrimping after money?"

"No, that was never him at all. That's where he was different. He knew his obligations and he stuck to them, but he never—never—never neglected his family. We were number one and we knew it."

"Yeah, fine."

"That's true."

"Sure."

"Well, it is."

They sat silently then, like two strangers next to each other on a green vinyl bus seat. From the first moment of their retreat, the active, all-encompassing silence of the park crept over them, like a recrimination.

"Oh, Laurel, what are we arguing about?"

"I don't know."

"I don't know, either. I don't."

He squeezed her then, and his arm encountered a stiffened body becoming slowly pliant beneath his shoulder. His own body melted in with hers.

"I'm sorry," he said spontaneously.

"Me too," she whispered.

As she settled close to him, her warmth touched something else within him, something dormant, and something that rushed out to meet her. When they kissed, it was such a wet and careless kiss that he felt himself engulfed by it, much as a lost sailor might feel himself welcomed by a dark, final whirlpool at the very end of the ocean. He forgot his breath and let himself be drawn slowly and succulently inward. He settled into his love and, for the time being, wallowed in it.

Despite their argument, he loved her.

He loved her.

Even after their argument, he fell quickly and completely back in love with her. And he thought then, and later, of making love to her, of doing everything with her, everything a boy could do with a girl. Yet their whole love was still so new and exciting that whatever they did with each other when they were together was miraculous. He loved being with her.

He did not, however, enjoy being without her at all. When he was alone, and thinking of her, his imagination would often take a painful turn into the past. He would think of the others she must have touched that way, the other boys she must have surprised with her sure hand on their legs. It was not difficult, then, to imagine how she must have also made these earlier boys shiver when she held them and squeezed them through their thin cotton pants in a passionate night. He had visions of Laurel and her blond handsome lovers in Southern California situations: backseats and theaters and beaches, where the swimsuits must have made it so easy for them.

He knew these scenes belonged only to his imagination, but they tied him in knots nonetheless. His imagination had taken things that might have happened long ago and made them real in the present. It was mortifying, but he couldn't free himself from it. He wanted to avoid thinking of her past, but he couldn't. The only alternative would be to ask her about it, but this was also dangerous. He knew from the confident way she acted that at least a part of his nightmare had been reality, and this was the part he wanted to spare himself.

It wasn't like that when he was with her. When they were together it seemed that all his doubts were quelled and shown to be the transparent constructions they were. All his sad and twisted visions were shattered and blown to smoke, simply by her company. There was no doubt of her love then, and there seemed no necessity that she even have a past at all. Everything was now.

But then, when she left, he would slide back. Once, when he was alone and attempting to amuse himself, he picked up an article on sex surrogates, women who treat men with sexual problems. The article was an interview with a sex surrogate and she described her method. It involved a lot of mutual nakedness and squeezing and controlled ejaculation and various other things. The men would come by appointment, get squeezed and all that, finally working up to balling, if there was still time left in the hour. It was all very professional and ho-hum, but Frankie could tell by the end of the first paragraph that the story was going to tie him in knots. He didn't even know the woman they were interviewing, she had nothing to do with him. She had nothing to do with Laurel, either, and yet the story did nothing but tie him in knots.

It was such a debilitating response. He found himself wishing that Laurel had no past, that he had no past, that the world had no past. In fact, he found he could solve the whole problem by wishing simply that there were no world.

Not a very realistic solution.

It wasn't very smart, letting Laurel's past or the sex surrogate's professional caresses get to him so, but it was a swift and unconscious reaction. It had something to do with his desire to find the world that he encountered to be as pure and faithful as he must have hoped it would be. And that just wasn't realistic—he knew that.

Still, these things tied him in knots. It was like some black-eyed Romantic demon in his bones. He couldn't get rid of it.

When he wasn't thus occupied wishing that the world would disappear, Frankie managed to visit it from time to time, at Lopez, or at the Prayerbook court. He kept in touch. On Friday afternoon, near Lopez, he met Billy Lyons.

"Frankie."

"Billy. What's happening?"

Billy wrapped his arm over Frankie's shoulder and pulled him into a private distance. "Frankie," he whispered, "it's tonight."

"What is?"

"The caper, man, the caper."

"Oh, yeah, the caper. What's the story, anyway?"

"Okay." Billy checked the surrounding area quickly, to be sure their conversation would be private.

"Look, it's all set. Sonny's got everything ready. We're just going along for the ride, man, really."

Frankie wasn't completely certain that this would be a ride he might want to take. "Wait a second, Billy. You never told me what it is your brother's got planned, anyway."

Billy chuckled merrily and rubbed his hands together. "Frankie, man, you're never going to believe it."

His laughter was infectious; Frankie was grinning when he asked, "Come on, tell me, tell me, huh?"

"Okay. Okay." Billy took time to calm himself. "This is it. Ah, the plan is to . . . ah . . . steal a buffalo."

"Steal a buffalo?"

"Yeah, yeah, right." Billy was cracking up again; he had to force himself to come back down to earth. "Sonny's got it all planned. The way he figures it, he lifts the buffalo, gets it home, him and his old lady carves it up, you know, and they store it in their freezer and have free meat all summer. Sonny says he'll be goddamned if he'll pay the prices they're charging at the supermarkets."

"Yeah, but Billy . . . ?"

"No, listen, it's all set. He's got everything figured. He's even going to use the hides to make seat covers for his Ford."

"Where are you planning to get the buffalo, from a pet store?"

"No, no, from the park, man, from the park."

That's right, Frankie thought, from the park. There they were, just standing around there, waiting to be wrapped up and taken home. All of a sudden it

seemed that Sonny's crazy-ass plan might even be for
real. But it was still the most unusual idea he'd heard
in a long time—and here he was, going along with it.

"Billy, look, you sure he's got everything set? I
mean, like, he's going to get the buffalo . . . How's he
going to get the thing from the park to his house? The
bastards must weigh a couple of tons."

"All set, all set. He's got the truck from work and
he rigged up a special setup on the back, strictly for
buffaloes."

"Oh yeah?"

"Yeah, and a special canvas cover so that we don't
attract too much attention driving down Potrero, you
know?"

"I see, I see."

"Right. And the thing is, he doesn't really need us,
but I wouldn't miss going along for the ride for anything, would you?"

"No," said Frankie. What else could he say?

"Good, good." Billy licked his lips and resumed
speaking. "Sonny and I'll pick you up at eleven tonight,
right across the street here. You be waiting by the pole
there, okay?"

"Okay."

"Unbelievable. We're gonna steal a buffalo."

"Yeah." Unbelievable.

He broke the news to Laurel later in the day.

"A what?"

"A buffalo. They're over in the park."

"Sure, but . . . how do you steal a buffalo?"

"It's all set. Billy's brother is the one who's really going to do it. We're just going along for the ride."

"Oh."

"It ought to be, uh, interesting."

"Sure. Do they still shoot people for stealing buffaloes?"

"Shoot people? I don't know. I didn't know they ever did."

"Sure they did. Like horse thieves."

"You mean . . . ? Ah, Laurel, no, I don't think so. I don't think they do that anymore."

"Well, I hope not."

"No, look, it's no sweat, really. Billy's brother has the whole thing figured out. He's going to use the hides for seat covers."

"Seat covers?"

"Yeah, for his Ford."

Laurel laughed. "His car will smell like a dead buffalo."

Frankie laughed back. "A dead buffalo. Imagine hitching a ride and getting picked up by a car that smells like a dead buffalo?"

They dissolved into laughter then, as further scenes and complications came to mind.

"What about getting stopped by the Highway Patrol for a spot inspection?"

"Yeah," said Frankie, "how would they handle that? How do you flunk a car for smelling bad?"

"Air pollution."

They laughed again. Frankie came out of his laughter sputtering. "Hey, wait, wait. What about when he drives through the park and his car gets attacked by a wild buffalo in heat?"

"How do you explain that to the insurance man?"

"Description of accident: car buggered by horny buffalo."

Their laughter relieved some of Frankie's tension. He felt only good about himself and about the whole silly world that surrounded him. Being with Laurel just seemed to do that for him. When they'd finished their laughing, and she'd wished him luck, and they'd said good-bye, Frankie was left alone on the gray sidewalk like a child after a parade. Inside him were mingled the residual warmth of his enjoyment and the dull disorientation of the moment. He had to slap his fist into the palm of his other hand a few times to get himself together. Then he walked briskly home.

When neither Billy nor the truck had appeared by eleven, Frankie began to wonder. He'd been standing across the busy street from Lopez for nearly an hour and it began to look as if he'd been standing there in vain. His stomach had been a bit queasy when he'd first stationed himself next to the lamppost, but this unscheduled change of plans seemed to indicate that some unforeseen hitch had developed during the course of their adventure. In that case, he could relax—they probably weren't coming tonight.

It was then, of course, that they came, Billy and his brother in the flashing wrecker. He saw them at the last moment, as the truck screeched to a stop, belching smoke and noise, with its complement of colored lights on all sides, like a Christmas tree gone wild.

"Frankie, hop in."

He did, squeezing between Billy and the door. His brother slammed the truck into gear and they lurched off, rumbling and growling, into the traffic. With all their lights, the scene reminded Frankie of the *Titanic* on the night of the iceberg. He looked around for life rafts but there were none.

"Sorry we're late," said Billy. "We had some last-minute fixing to do on the rig."

"It's okay."

Billy and Frankie and the door bumped into each other regularly as the truck bounced and groaned in a painful second gear. Sonny was driving, hunched over the wheel like a vulture. The passing streetlights played slow tricks with his slicked-back ducktail hair. As was his custom, he said nothing, concentrating instead on some dark foreign point in the infinite distance. The word taciturn had been invented for Sonny.

"Whaddya think, man?" Billy was rubbing his hands again and smiling.

"I don't know."

"Here we go, Frankie, just like I told you, here we go."

Frankie was a little nervous again. "Yeah, here we go."

Once Sonny had built up a head of steam the loud clumsy wrecker fairly flew down the road. Frankie was surprised at the speed. He wondered how fast it could go with the weight of a dead buffalo hanging from the end.

"Here we go," said Billy, as Sonny began his turn.

"Here we go," Frankie answered automatically.

Sonny said nothing.

They turned into the park, where it was quite dark relative to the main drag, and Sonny somehow managed to extinguish all their garish lights save the necessary head- and taillights. It became immediately darker inside the cab of the truck. All eyes were directed outward, toward their prey.

(Frankie had read somewhere that Buffalo Bill had shot 69 buffalo in eight hours, which might have been the record or something. He did it in a contest, in which his opponent was able to dispatch only 50 or so to their eternal reward. Bill was the champ. Of course that left 119 or so buffalo to decompose in fly-infested heaps on the harsh prairie. Meanwhile, Indians died of starvation, or something like that. Whatever the specifics, Frankie remembered that he felt only revulsion upon hearing the story. Now, here he was, on a buffalo hunt. One thing he had in his favor, though, was that the buffalo would not be allowed to decompose in a vulture-ridden desert. It would be used. All of it. They'd probably make salad forks out of its bones.)

They pulled to the side of the road near the field where the buffalo roamed, albeit constrictedly. There was no movement, no sign of anyone in the area. An occasional car wandered by on Kennedy Drive, but they would never notice. Sonny rotated the small spotlight from the driver's side of the cab and, as Frankie's eyes became accustomed to it, he could pick out the dark buffalo figures like blemishes against the gray landscape. They weren't moving.

Sonny opened the door and hopped out of the cab.

Frankie resisted an urge to do something and nervously sat there. Sonny was fumbling with something in the space down behind the cab. When he reappeared he was carrying a rifle, loading it with large brass shells. Frankie heard the click as they snapped into the cold snug chamber.

"Should we get out?" he whispered to Billy.

"No. We stay here for now."

They stayed and watched Sonny as he advanced into the searchlight's weak gaze. He carried the rifle at his hip and walked quietly toward the nearest animal, which was standing just to the other side of the low, camouflaged barrier. Frankie watched as Sonny lifted each leg and carefully put it down, tracking his prey like an Indian hunter. He was even wearing moccasins. He would have looked authentic but for his shining duck-tail haircut and his dungaree jacket with the multicolored sequins on the back, spelling out SONNY in ticklish flashes.

This buffalo, like all the other buffalo Frankie could see, was standing dumbly in the grassy field. His head hung down toward his knees, as if it were too heavy for his neck to support. His fur was spotted, or missing in spots, and his tail was limp. As Sonny approached, the buffalo remained motionless, in profile. His slow white eye stared out from the side of his monumental head. He looked sad, or bored, or both.

Sonny raised the rifle, aimed at the eye, pulled the trigger, and the entire park seemed suddenly filled with the one large sound.

The buffalo waited for a time before falling in a

heap, dead. As for his fellows, they scarcely stirred before returning to their stonelike, dazed existence. They neither knew nor cared.

Sonny hesitated in the aftermath, awaiting a reaction that never came. When the sound had died away, he spurred himself into action, loping back toward the truck. He threw the rifle in the back and climbed into the cab.

"You got him," Billy said.

Sonny said nothing. Instead he kicked the truck into motion, wheeling it forward and to the right, preparing to back toward the buffalo. He slammed the transmission into reverse and the truck leaped back toward the pile of meat and hide. The brakes squeaked two or three times, throwing Frankie backward, until they felt a slight bump as the rear of the truck touched the barrier. Sonny abruptly disengaged the clutch and yanked the emergency brake up into position. In a flash he was out of the cab and at the back of the truck.

"Should we get out?" Frankie asked again.

"Yeah, let's get out."

Frankie opened the door. Its parched croak echoed in the forest.

"Get back in there!" Sonny shouted, and they obeyed. The door gave a short, high-pitched squeak as Frankie slammed it shut.

He couldn't prevent their looking through the back window, though, which they did, and they watched as he went quickly about his business with the buffalo. The motor on the lift whined as he let out the hook, and stopped as he attached it to the buffalo's head. The winch whined again, and then groaned as the buffalo's weight began to be dragged and finally hefted slowly from the cold ground. It was an inch-by-inch process, until the buffalo's head appeared at last upon the truck's horizon. There followed the broad, furry neck and the upper torso. The winch clinked to a stop, and locked, with the massive head straining upward, toward the dark sky, at the very top of the lift.

Sonny unfurled the canvas cover and snapped it together at the top of the lift, and down the sides, until it covered the carcass of the buffalo like a teepee. Now they were in the clear; they would seem to be only a wrecker towing a teepee. Nothing unusual about that.

Sonny stood back for one more look at his work before rushing back to the cab.

"Great, Sonny," said Billy.

"Looks good," said Frankie.

Sonny glanced at them quickly, revealing nothing. He threw the truck into gear and they were off.

It was clear from the first that there was something heavy and breakable on the back. Sonny drove as if he were driving over eggs. He inched his way out onto Fulton Street and they were on their way. There wasn't much traffic but Sonny still seemed nervous, glancing frequently at the mirror and over his shoulder. But he said nothing. Nor did either Billy or Frankie.

They were making good time and were over the hump, heading downhill, when the presence of a flashing blue light intruded suddenly, competing with their own orange flasher against the surrounding buildings. Immediately they stiffened. Sonny was obviously playing it cool, refusing to panic, until he heard the siren warning the cars behind them to move. Then he panicked.

He jumped on the accelerator and they took off, running with gas and gravity down the hill. Frankie and Billy held on to the dashboard. They switched their attention rapidly from the front to the back, and to the front again, unclear as to which direction presented the greatest and most immediate danger. Frankie soon decided it was the front.

Sonny's driving was wild, careening through three lanes, bouncing from hill to hill, and sailing off the plateaux created by the cross streets like a ski jumper. The traffic in front of them parted before their lights and sirens like the Red Sea before a charging, roaring prophet. It was unreal. The police car was gaining on them, finally holding steady at about ten yards behind them. From there it followed, perhaps it crept toward them a bit, it was hard to tell in the rocking, diving cab.

There was no fear. There was only a suspension of feeling. Sonny bit his lip through in the effort of his concentration. Billy and Frankie were suspended in time. The police car clung to them like some evil insect.

They were almost to the bottom of the hill, and travelling at an alarming rate, when they hit a particularly severe depression. All three passengers were shaken by the impact of the wheels and the shocks on the suddenly level ground. It was a bone-shattering crunch, as if the hard asphalt had come up to meet them at sixty miles an hour.

The buffalo didn't make it. They felt his absence

immediately and turned to see what had happened just as the blue-flashing police car plowed into the bouncing buffalo at sixty miles an hour. There was a definite crash. The police car's lights lurched up in the air and bounced back down before being suddenly extinguished by yet another crash. The last thing they saw was the car rolling slowly, hesitantly, on its side, down the hill.

They drove quickly and silently through the dark streets to Sonny's house on Potrero Hill. They parked the truck in the driveway and disappeared, each in his own direction, without a word to explain themselves. It was quite clear, in an abstracted, unreal sort of way, that they were each of them scared. But so did they each of them exhibit the beatitude of extreme situations, that peaceful sense of removal which makes the most sudden and dangerous of things into an accomplished fact. Something that can be handled, something that can be accepted. There was nothing, certainly, to do but wait. With crossed fingers perhaps. Meanwhile the dream world continued, faintly desiring release, to be granted only in the inevitable, suitably violent, dawn.

PART

The players flowed up and down the court like water sluicing back and forth in a gold miner's flat pan. The game was underway, sure and mechanical.

It was four-on-four, comprising the entire cast of Prayerbook players. Frankie was teamed with Clyde and Jimmy and Number 44. Once they had broken a sweat, the game proceeded with a pulsing regularity, accentuated by the rushing of rubber-soled feet toward first the one end, then the other. Each cycle would reach its climax, its point of highest activity, just as all feet left the ground and a moment of precipitous silence warned that the basket would be made or missed, and the process would be repeated.

Frankie spent most of his time under the boards. His shot of choice was a fall-away jump shot, when it was open, but it was rare that he found himself in position to shoot. Most often he would be at the basket during that moment of suspension, poised to return an errant shot toward the waiting steel rim. The baskets were constructed of steel and chain, and a perfect set shot finished with a distinctive *chink* as the metal net caught and gently dropped the ball to the concrete. Most shots were not perfect, and the most common sound was a disorganized clattering, as if the basket were shaken unexpectedly from a dull sleep.

They had once kept a running score in their games, but this practice had been long since abandoned. There was only the game itself now, the smoothly accelerated motion flowing back and forth on the black asphalt rectangle.

It was not difficult for Frankie to lose himself in the game's rhythms. They seemed to echo those of his own body, its cycles of rushing and pausing, rushing and pausing, back and forth, again and again. Only rarely did he reflect on the article in the morning's *Chronicle,* with the picture of the shattered police car. One of the cops was close to death. Manslaughter.

He glanced over his shoulder at Number 44, who

was bringing the ball up with a confident and deceptive calm. The ball rose and fell at his fingertips like a magical extension of his arm, like something over which only he would ever have such a firm but leisurely control. All at once his rhythm altered, ever so slightly, and the ball came rushing toward Frankie, who watched it grow larger as it approached, and met with it on the dead run just two steps from the basket. His body responded perfectly, two counts, pushing firmly up and off on the last count, listening once again to the straining silence, and laying the ball softly over the gray rim and into the basket. Two points.

Number 44 was an enigmatic sort. He was a small, quick, black kid, who either owned but one shirt or else owned a lot of them, all with the same 44 across the front and back. Maybe he was a numerology freak. Four next to four. Even if that were the case, it would be impossible to confirm it, since he never talked to anyone, not even to the other black kids with whom he met every day to play basketball. The kid was a real mystery. No one in the group went in for much small talk, but some at least was expected, a phrase or a greeting here and there. Who would miss that? Only Number 44 stood reserved; he was silent.

There had been no word on arrests. It was only a matter of time. They might even be at his apartment. He should go home, so he could be there if they came. His mother would probably know what to do.

Frankie lay back and concentrated on defense for a while. The other team seemed to have entered a long shooting phase of its game, which limited Frankie's options to rebounding and goaltending. The latter was illegal, and the former was an infrequent choice, since so many shots either went in or reverberated off the backboard and rim almost to the backcourt. He glided and waited for the game to move into whatever its next phase might be.

On offense, Clyde was suddenly so hot with his jumper that they just fed him the ball and watched him throw it in. They listened to the sound of his baskets. *Chink. Chink.*

He hadn't told Laurel. He hadn't talked to Billy. It would be such a relief to have this trance of waiting ended.

Number 44 surprised everyone by continuing his advance up the court directly to the basket. He laid it in. No one ever knew what his real name was. He showed no emotion, no satisfaction, but backpedalled immediately to a defensive position.

Frankie knew that he would probably have to spend some time downtown. He might even have to spend that time in a cell. It would be bad news all around. But in the end he didn't think that he'd be liable for prosecution. After all, he was only a passenger.

Unless his very presence was all that was required for him to be guilty. Accessory before, during, and after the fact.

Manslaughter.

But he was a minor. They couldn't do that much to him, really. Could they?

He'd soon find out.

Frankie got the chance he'd been quietly awaiting

and he lofted a fall-away jump shot effortlessly toward the chain cradle. *Chink.*

What would jail be like?

Why had he ever agreed to be a part of something so cruel and foolish?

Why had it never occurred to him to ask himself these questions *before* the incident? It was too late now.

Frankie bobbled a pass and lost his timing, banking the layup too low off the backboard. He tried to recover for the rebound, but Leroy's thin, skeletal hand intercepted the basketball while Frankie could only watch. It was an effort to reverse direction and head back down court. His recovery was cut short when Clyde blocked a shot and sent a front-running Frankie off on a break. He stuffed the lay-up, shaking the basket and causing the chain to bounce right up through the hoop. He felt a little better after that.

All his thoughts of jail and prison bars brought to mind scenes from the dozens of Grade B prison flicks he'd seen over the years. Movies with John Garfield and James Cagney standing tough against the wardens and guards and gutless governors of the world. How come they always had to get the Garfields and Cagneys in the end? They always had to be killed, either violently or while spitting calmly in the warden's eye.

That was how they became heroes. By dying. By being abandoned.

It all seemed kind of sick when you thought about it. Like the Roman Colosseum or something, where confused foreign gladiators played out their game in a ring of blood-stained lion shit. Thousands cheered as the animals chomped on the remnants of an unfamiliar leg. Some hero.

Frankie's mind produced something for a wall.

> I'm no hunter
> I'm no hero
> I'm no gladiator
> I'm a lion lover
> —the shadow

He didn't even look for the ball and missed a pass from Number 44. Jimmy retrieved the ball as Frankie stood by himself at the corner of the court. It was suddenly very clear that his life had been irrecoverably altered and that he was going to have to come to terms with it. Everything would change. It might be for the better, or for the worse, but it would be different. He watched, in a dreamlike way, as Jimmy came running back with the ball tucked under his arm.

It could have been just another aspect of the dream which saw Billy Lyons emerge from his camouflage behind a bush. He summoned Frankie with a gesture.

"What is it?"

"Come here." Billy pulled them both back into the shelter of the rambling bush. "Let's stay out of sight."

"Okay."

Billy observed a moment of silence, waiting for some internal signal that all was clear. Evidently he got it, because he relaxed noticeably and showed Frankie a smile that reminded him of the way he'd looked when he'd first announced the buffalo plan.

"What is it, Billy?"

"Frankie, dig it, everything's gonna be okay."

"Okay?"

"Yeah, man, copasetic."

"What are you talking about? It's manslaughter, for Christ's sake."

"Sssh." Billy raised a finger to his lips. "Cool it, cool it. It's gonna be all right."

Frankie whispered, "But what about the cop?"

Billy scowled. "Fuck him, Frankie, that was just a big scam. He's healthier than any of us. They just do that shit for the papers."

"Yeah, but . . ."

"Okay, listen, here's the story. They got Sonny."

"They got Sonny! Oh, that's just fucking great all right, just what we need."

"Will you relax, Frankie? Like I told you, it's gonna be okay."

"What's gonna be okay? What about us?"

"We're gonna be all right."

"We are?"

"Sure. Sonny won't tell them nothing."

"You sure?"

"Of course I'm sure. He's my brother, right? I know him."

"Yeah?"

"Course. Besides, he already claimed he knows nothing about it and he's gonna stick to that story. He's got a lawyer. He'll be okay."

"You think so?"

"I know it. Sonny always lands standing up."

"How'd they find him so quick?"

"Ah, well, you know. They got the number off the truck."

"Oh."

"They traced it to the garage and then to him."

"Right."

"So they caught him with it in the driveway."

"What'd they do?"

"Ah, well, he claimed it had never left the house. Must have been some mistake. He was giving them the big line, you know, that he'd been there all night with witnesses to prove it, and then the cops told him to get his lawyer because they were taking him downtown."

"How come?"

"Because they found the damn buffalo's jawbone still stuck to the hook."

"Oh. Doesn't look too good then, huh?"

"Shit, don't worry about Sonny. He'll get off. He's gonna claim the truck was stolen. Or else that somebody planted the evidence on the hook. The heat's been known to do that, you know? He'll get off."

Frankie nodded and began to gravitate back to his game. Billy noticed and responded by pulling off in the opposite direction. "So it's all set, Frankie, no sweat."

"No sweat."

"Just forget all about it and we'll make out okay."

Frankie nodded.

Billy stopped and smiled, pointing at Frankie to emphasize his parting comment: "Just make believe it never even happened at all, and we'll be in the clear."

Frankie nodded and walked slowly back to the game.

When the game broke up, its players dribbling off individually in their separate directions, Frankie went north, toward Fulton Street. It was the middle of the afternoon, the brightest, most unreal part of the day, and he felt he needed the walk to clear his head. It was Saturday and the streets were temporarily quiet, waiting for the bustle to come, when the ball games ended and the picnics and the drives to Marin and San Jose were completed.

Frankie walked east, with his own shadow just barely ahead of him. To his right, the gray, craggy, stone wall slid past, broken by tufts of derelict grass which spilled out through cracks in the tired cement. The rocks were more black than gray, showing their age.

He'd heard somewhere that the entire park had been sand and rock at one time, an infertile dune upon which the present coating of green and gold had been superimposed. He'd also heard that the sand and stone had begun to resurface, gradually, starting out at the beach, and that it was making its way slowly eastward, to reclaim its rightful domain. It wouldn't have seemed possible in the sunny morning, but in the metallic glare of the afternoon he could almost feel the dry shifting sand following behind him.

It reminded him of a poem by Shelley which he couldn't quite remember.

There were spots of white on the dark wall, put there by hasty paintbrushes over the years. Alphabet soup, mostly. Things like JB + LM, FO + JJ, MH + BB. Or else one weather-worn JIMI! whose cry of desperation remained. Other names, which might have been those of gangs or clubs, appeared occasionally, but mostly it was letters. Romeo and Juliet in the crumbling concrete.

Frankie had no white pen with him. In fact he had only one color with him, black, but he did have his penknife. Squatting before the wall, he put the penknife to work, etching into the dark rock

> Call me when the sand gets to here
> —the shadow

but it was hard work and unrewarding. When he finished and looked back, the thing was barely perceptible. He left it there, as a small reminder, and continued on his way. A bus, heading downtown, caught up with him and he got on.

There were only five or six people on the entire bus. He chose a seat near the back and settled in next to the window. The park, and its crumbling wall, ran by more quickly than before.

The people inside the bus rocked back and forth in unison. They closed their eyes, and opened them on bumps, letting them fall gradually shut again as the bus rolled on. Some glanced unconsciously at the inside of the bus and at the other passengers, being careful just the same to ensure that their eyes should not meet. An old man with a Hitler-style mustache who was sitting facing the aisle at the front of the bus kept peeking back to look at Frankie. He always looked away when Frankie's eyes turned his way. Eventually, Frankie took to staring at him, which disturbed him no end. At last he exited the bus suddenly (Frankie was sure that it wasn't even his stop) and Frankie was left, in his seat at the back, the sole male passenger. The old women paid him no attention, as long as he behaved himself.

Whether from boredom, or restlessness, or just the continued presence of the penknife in his hand, Frankie began to use it on the back of the seat in front of him. He started by scraping the letter W into the green metal. The sound was loud and horrible, like fingernails across a blackboard. The woman seated two seats in front of him turned and peered back over her shoulder. Frankie smiled at her and stopped scraping.

He was only about halfway through the letter W, but he still had no final notion of what it was that he wanted to write. He fingered the penknife and considered

Whaaat?
—the shadow

or

Why?
—the shadow

or even

Why not?
—the shadow

but none of these seemed to carry any real purpose. There was nothing there.

Finally he unleashed his knife and finished the W, scraping obscenely, and signed it

W
—the shadow

When he looked up, the woman was regarding him with unrestrained curiosity. He glared at her. She dismissed him with a shake of her head and turned to the front. Frankie closed up his knife and put it away.

He thought of the subways in New York, with their wild, unfettered, uptown coloring. Huge, sinuous drawings on the sides of the silver cars. Always the names only, though, the first name or the nickname, and the number of the street from which the artist came. Their motives must have been a little different from his, although he couldn't quite put his finger on it. Maybe they just substituted color for content. Or maybe they tried to blow up their names to include all the questions and comments which Frankie took such pains to articulate. Or else maybe they were just behind him—or ahead of him. What the hell, he didn't know.

New York. It was like a different world. All that darkness and all those silver trains sliding through the arteries of the earth like speckled lizards through tunnels in the ground. New York. It was like Mars.

The bus continued on its squeaky way toward Market Street and downtown. Its passengers remained quiet beneath the shroud of electric silence. Frankie read the ads.

There's a New Today Army Waiting
for You!

Great.

Psoriasis Is Not a Social Disease.

> *It's antisocial, right? Isn't it?*
> *All sorts of scales and things?*

Double Your Pleasure
Double Your Fun!

> *Use two hands.*

Learn Computer Programming at
Home.

> *Sure thing. Providing you have your*
> *own personal computer to work on.*
> *If not, sign here. Get screwed by a*
> *UNIVAC or an ELECTROLUX*
> *rather than by a common human.*

Find God
Write Box 33
Mission Station

Don't Wait
Do It Now!

> *Beautiful. A P.O. box.*

The bus rolled and lurched toward flat land. They
passed over the street where last night they had lost the
buffalo, and where the police car had crashed. There
was no sign of an accident. There was nothing really to
indicate that anything at all unusual had happened at

that intersection on the previous night. Less than twenty-four hours before. No blood or wreckage whatsoever. Not even any unreclaimed glass, nothing to glint secretly from the gutter to the passing bus, to mark the spot of a past disaster. Nothing.

It was almost as if it hadn't happened.

What had Billy said? Something like, Just forget it ever happened. Just forget it.

Apparently that even cleaned up the gutters. Mind over matter.

He got off the bus at Market Street and wandered downtown, where there were more people than were out by the park, but where the same silence seemed to have penetrated and engulfed everything. The people walked briskly to and fro on the broad sidewalk, intent upon their shopping or whatever it was they were up to, but they were unusually quiet about it. The whole scene was eerie. Even the cars were slow and noiseless as they maneuvered around the wreckage left by the BART construction. The faces of the shoppers seemed as uniform and expressionless as those of an army at drill. Frankie listened and could hear the clicking of their heels all around him. Long, confident strides in syncopated patterns on the concrete. Eerie.

His own pace slowed, dulled by the squashed soundlessness of his sneakers, and he ceased his walking altogether by the green signal box at the corner of Third Street. The stream of tight-lipped shoppers, and the shy traffic, flowed around him.

He toyed with the penknife in his pocket and watched the cars. They stopped and started, pausing now and then to permit a group of shoppers to pass, before gliding forward through the intersection. Buses pulled up regularly, hissing and creaking. The doors flapped open and yet another contingent of wide-eyed shoppers was discharged.

There was no way he could believe that the whole thing was all over with, done with. Over and forgotten. As if it had never happened. Someone had almost died, or had been thought by many to be almost dead, and now they were in the clear. But things just don't go that way.

And yet, there it was. Billy had said that Sonny wouldn't talk and, knowing only as much about Sonny as he did, Frankie was sure that he would not. It would be in Sonny's character to go it alone. Like John Wayne, or James Cagney, or . . . John Garfield.

Sonny wouldn't break, that much was certain. Whatever they might threaten him with, he'd smile and say, Go ahead, give me your best shot. He wouldn't give them the satisfaction of seeing him break down.

So Frankie and Billy were off the hook, so to speak. Just like the buffalo.

He had an urge to take a walk down by the jail, just to look at it, but he resisted it, since he really wasn't quite sure where it was. It was right down by the police station, wasn't it? The Hall of Justice? On Harrison or Bryant somewhere. He could have looked it up, but there was no sense in it. He leaned back against the pole.

Normally, things weren't this quiet when one had just been let off the hook. There should be some sort of demonstration or celebration or something. Some sort of noise. Instead he was relegated to secrecy and quiet and to the unmistakable feeling that he had been condemned to something rather than freed from it.

It was probably the company of these Market Street zombies as much as anything else. And the sun-stained silence of the afternoon.

He took out his penknife and began to work on the green paint of the traffic signal. He etched away on the flat surface of the control box. Inside, the machine registered its complaint by means of a dull clunk, at regular intervals. The defacement was done in plain sight of everyone, but there was no need to worry that they might be at all upset about it, or about anything. He wanted to write the most uncomplicated, the most natural, the most hopeful thing he could. When he realized what it would be, he felt so silly, so embarrassed really, that he actually blushed as he scraped it on.

Frankie

+

Laurel

He didn't even need to sign it.

The coupled names looked so precious there, on the scuffed and weatherworn green metal. His scraping had revealed the shiny surface beneath and the names shone forth, bright silver.

Frankie

+

Laurel

There they were, out in the open, for everyone to see, even Laurel.

He looked back down Market and saw it immediately, painted huge and red as a comic book explosion, like a command this time, on the beige, windowless building:

action

He stuffed his hand in his pocket for a dime and skipped sideways across the street to the phone. The cars were too slow to hurt him even if they hit him.

He glided up to the booth and dialed Laurel's number. 555–8404. Sometimes the feeling of love wells up so suddenly and so completely from within you that it washes out all the weak, tired thoughts that had seemed so important the moment before. Frankie felt completely washed away. His only feeling was that of hunger, of a yearning from somewhere within him which he just knew would be satisfied by the sound of her voice. She picked up the phone and answered and it was.

"Laurel."

"Frankie."

"Hi."

While he melted into the phone, she flew toward him from her end, relieved and compassionate. "Are you all right? I've been so worried since I saw the paper."

"I'm fine. I'm fine."

"Oh I'm so glad. You don't know. Why didn't you call me earlier?"

"I didn't have a chance."

"Oh but you should have."

"I just found out for sure what happened. I wasn't really sure."

"Well, what happened? Tell me everything."

Frankie was pleased to hear the inflection of concern in her voice. He was pleased that she had been worried over him, that she had expected him to call right away. He wanted to tell her everything, but later, at their celebration, their own demonstration.

"I will, Laurel, but let's get together and talk about it. There's a lot to say. And we probably should celebrate or something, that things turned out as well as they did."

"Oh, you bet we should. Are you all right then?"

"Fine. I'm off the hook."

"Oh, good, good."

"So I guess we should celebrate."

"You bet. And you'd better tell me everything, Frankie O'Day, because you've got me almost crazy with the suspense."

Frankie laughed happily. "Everything, everything."

Their mouths tried to meet through the phone, but had to be satisfied with the squawk of electronic kisses. He wanted so much to make love to her, all the way, to be surrounded and soothed by her, tonight they would do it. He could feel it. It was so obvious that even the zombies on the street must have spotted it.

"So it'll be tonight," he said.

"Okay."

"I can't wait."

"Me neither."

"It'll be so good to be with you."

"So good."

"I'll see you then, honey."

"See you then, baby."

"See ya."

"See ya."

Frankie popped out right after supper and stopped by the Gateway Market for a pint of vodka. It was a celebration, certainly, and vodka was just the thing to celebrate with. You'd have your fun and no one could smell it on your breath. Or so they say.

He'd been getting served at the Gateway since he was fourteen. He and the proprietor had an agreement. They would nod pleasantly to each other and transact their business in the most laconic fashion possible. Frankie thought that was the adult way to handle things. His height was undoubtedly an important factor; either he looked old enough to drink, or else the old guy thought that he was too big to argue with.

Frankie paid him and left. He picked up two quarts of orange juice and some large paper cups at Lopez. J.T. was there, standing outside with the Lactus twins at his feet.

"Frankie, hey, where you going?"

"Nowhere. Just home."

"You coming back out?" J.T. inspected the brown bags which held the booze and orange juice. Heaven only knew what he was thinking.

"I don't know. Maybe later."

"How late?"

"I don't know. Nine or ten." Or eleven or twelve or . . .

"How come so late? Hey, I'm not going to be around then but I was hoping we might get a few beers before that."

"Ah, well, I don't know. I don't think I can make it."

"That's too bad, Frankie, I can't stick around 'til later."

Frankie asked, "Why not?" as if he really cared.

"I gotta get laid. You understand. It's been a week."

There's a future Jesuit for you, Frankie thought and laughed. He felt suddenly very warm and con- spiratorial at the knowledge that, whatever it was that would pass between Laurel and him that night, it would be their secret, their thing. He couldn't imagine telling anyone else in the world about it. It was beautiful.

"Sorry, J.T., maybe I'll catch you tomorrow."

"Sure. See you tomorrow."

Frankie practically ran down Lincoln Way toward their spot in the park. He took the fence with a high jumper's sidesaddle leap and jogged quickly up the path toward the top of the hill. He nestled the two bags against the big tree and surveyed the area with a glance. His heart danced in his chest like a little boy's.

As he walked away, the weight of a great and important event bore down upon him. He wondered if she was a virgin? He wondered if she knew, at that time, in her house, of his desire? He wondered if she would feel that way toward him? What if she refused? Could he bring himself to smile and laugh it off as if it had meant nothing at all to him?

What if she refused?

It was then that Frankie had his first temptation to call the whole thing off. Play it safe. Run away. Smile and avoid everything. Following that came a vision of Laurel waiting, like an imprisoned angel, in her room. His butterfly heart stopped, and melted completely away.

Standing across from Laurel's house, Frankie watched the sky grow warm and orange in the distance. It was so momentarily bright that it placed Laurel's square quiet house in relative darkness. There were no lights on inside, and it wasn't possible to distinguish any forms or figures through the half-shrouded windows. They must have finished their dinner. Her father and her brother would be in the sunken living room watching TV. Some news program probably. Her mother would be in the kitchen washing the dishes. Laurel would be in her room; with luck, she would be almost ready to go.

He crossed quickly to her porch and rang her doorbell. There was a sudden rustling at the inside of the door and it opened, showing Laurel, herself, in her starched cleanliness, with her hand on the knob. She called her good-byes and received her instructions over her shoulder, so Frankie didn't even have to go in. When she finally pulled the Spanish door shut behind her, and he heard its heavy, telltale click, Frankie was so buoyantly relieved that he could have leaped from the stone porch out to the darkening street. And he could have carried Laurel with him.

They bumped into each other pleasantly as they walked. Frankie found that he was physically excited by her very proximity, and each touch of their walking bodies through their clothes seemed to strengthen the magnetism by which they were already drawn together. So did they walk, bouncing and rubbing against each other, springing toward their place in the park.

It was hard to walk, he was so excited. It was equally hard to pay much attention to Laurel's repeated commentary on the good fortune by which he'd escaped punishment in the buffalo debacle. He forced himself to tell her everything, in response to her questioning, and he longed for the safety and darkness of the hill in the park. What he really wanted to do was to kiss and hold her, but he had to wait for the leafy protection of the park.

Once inside, she melted into his arms. He kissed her and forced himself against her like a spiteful child, hurt and impatient with the waiting. She moved with him, like a dancer, and fit perfectly in everything he did. When they parted at last, he helped her out of her jacket, since it was warm, and her young, perfect body called to him from beneath the starched shirt and the crisp jeans, but he forced himself to wait long enough for the urge to continue undressing her to pass. To assist in submerging his desire, he spoke. "I like your jacket." It was small and heavy and smelled like leather.

"Thanks. Daddy got it for me at Neiman-Marcus. That's like I. Magnin's up here. They really have beautiful stuff."

"Yeah, it's really nice."

"I made him get it while it was on sale, too. One thing you'll find about me, Frankie O'Day, is that I know how to shop. I never buy anything, anything, unless I can get a deal on it." She smiled.

Frankie raised his eyebrows. "Beautiful. What do you want to be when you grow up? The Consumer Protection Agency?"

Laurel laughed and gave him a playful jab. He parried it automatically and surrounded her arms with his own. They kissed and smiled at each other.

Still holding her jacket, he stepped back and reached around behind her to lay it gently on the pine carpet. When he returned he touched her softly, along her front and sides. Her small, nippled breasts lay quiet and uncovered beneath the cotton. They were suddenly so warm and unpretentious it surprised him. He touched them reverently. She smiled back at him, with her sparkling teeth and eyes, and reached directly to his most swollen and defenseless part, grasping and squeezing him with her hand.

Frankie was attached to her then, like a puppet at the direction of her practiced touch, and it was a feeling which always excited him, which brought the blood pounding ever more helplessly in his veins. He looked into her smiling face, where her top teeth were pressed into her lower lip in that coquettish fashion of hers, and he found he was grinning himself, like a dribbling fool at a magical shop window. What else could she do to him? It was amazing.

Nothing—nothing—could be as pleasurable as this.

He thought about coming inside her and he wondered if even that could surpass the tactile enjoyment which presently possessed him. It was difficult to imagine. He stared into her face, so familiar as an object of his longing, and so irrecoverable in her absence, and kissed her softly.

"Laurel"—he wanted to say I love you—"tonight we have to celebrate."

She beamed back at him. "You bet we do."

"Uhm, and here's the surprise," he said, removing his hands from her sides and leaning toward his cache in the bags by the tree.

"What is it?"

"It's a celebration surprise." He fumbled with the bag and drew out the bottle, and then the cartons of orange juice and the cups, one by one.

"Oh ho," said Laurel. "This *is* a celebration, isn't it."

"That's right," said Frankie, brandishing the pint of clear liquid. "A celebration all the way."

Laurel smiled and raised her eyebrows.

Frankie announced, "Vodka and orange juice."

"Screwdrivers," Laurel added.

"That's right. Good for your health, too. Would you care for one, my dear?"

"Why, certainly. I mean, it *is* a celebration, isn't it?"

"Right. We're celebrating the release of Frankie O'Day—yours truly—from the doom of imprisonment."

"Not to mention the awful publicity."

"Not to mention it."

Frankie began the ritual of measuring. First the clear liquid, faintly pungent, spilled from its viewless confinement to the flat, plastic freedom of the cup. Then came the orange inundation, which was never quite able to do with taste or with smell what it did with color. A stir of the finger (this was, after all, the outdoors—reason enough to rough it a bit) and they were ready.

"Here you go."

"Thank you."

She accepted the cup with no small measure of grace and stood facing him with her drink aloft, theatrically. Frankie smiled and began to drink, when she stopped him.

"Wait."

"What?"

"A toast." She smiled and turned her head, looking at him out of the sides of her eyes, a gentle reminder of something he'd so easily overlooked.

"A toast." He nodded his head agreeably. "Okay, what shall we toast to?"

"Well, how about, to us?"

He smiled. "To us."

"To us."

They raised their cups and drank, with their eyes holding fixed upon each other, maintaining their connection by rolling smoothly down and up as their heads tilted to receive the toast. Laurel licked her lips in the aftermath; Frankie smiled and felt his own lips wet and stinging slightly from the juice. The vodka made its presence felt first in his throat, then in his chest, at the point where the esophagus pours out into the yawning stomach.

Laurel laughed. "Good. A good mix."

"Thank you."

"Do you want to sit down?"

"Why not?"

Frankie assisted her, in a gentlemanly fashion, as she sat back against the tree. He lowered himself to a spot beside her, with his own back against the tree and his arm and shoulder against hers, until they were settled, making an angle of about five degrees with their outstretched legs. They held their milk shake cups in their laps and they drank from them, when they did, together, in goodly drafts, with their eyes turned toward each other.

The first few gulps produced only that unfortunate searing sensation at the top of the chest. It was that which caused their eyes to water so sentimentally. Once done, their early tears seemed to find just cause in their feeling for each other. He looked at her and smiled. Once again, he could almost have said, I love you. It was that close. It would come.

He recalled that earlier evening when he'd asked if she loved him. She'd paused and evaded and smiled and equivocated, but he was sure from her actions that she did. He was sure now that she did.

"I feel nice," she said.

"Me too."

It was just about as dark as it was going to get. The lights from the street were at their strongest, yet it was their distant benefaction which made the place so wonderful. As the light filtered through the shrubbery and the trees, there survived only enough to make each other visible against the surrounding darkness. They could look and see and laugh. They could peer out to the street and watch the foreign, garish crowds, rushing down the sidewalks to their foreign destinations. But they, themselves, could not be seen, save by each other. It was a friendly light.

Laurel reached around behind her for her coat. Without looking, she found the pocket and retrieved a package of cigarettes. They came in a burgundy-colored box. Frankie didn't recognize the brand.

"How about a cigarette, Frankie?"

"Ah, well, I don't know. I'm trying not to."

"Oh, come on. Tonight we're celebrating, remember?"

"Yeah."

"So have one."

"Okay." He reached and took the box from her. It was a brand he'd never seen before. Courtleigh. "What are these?"

"Oh, my father brought me those back from South Africa."

"Oh."

"He was there in the spring, working on some kind of a distribution thing I have absolutely no idea about."

"Oh."

"You can't get them here in the States, I guess."

"I guess not."

Frankie looked at the aristocratic velveteen box. On an impressive gold banner strung diagonally across the front was imprinted

COURTLEIGH—THE WORLD'S MOST EXCLUSIVE CIGARETTE

It looked quite strange there, balanced between the fingers of his outstretched hand. It made his fingernails seem dirty, but it must have been the shadow.

After some experimentation, he opened the box and a small piece of white paper fell out onto the ground. It looked like a guarantee, seal and all. He picked it up and read it.

> Courtleigh gold band filter cigarettes are hand blended from a unique stock of well-matured tobaccos which have been expertly selected for taste, flavour and aroma.
>
> COURTLEIGH
> THE WORLD'S MOST EXCLUSIVE CIGARETTE

He didn't know whether to take one or not. There they were, nestled like precious, dry, white infants in a golden-papered nursery. Each was crowned with a tiny gold band, like a pedigree, at the base of the filter tip. It was such a shame to disturb them. Hesitantly, he did, selecting one of the thin, white cylinders for smoking. Laurel lit it for him. It tasted like plastic.

Laurel was watching. "What do you think of them?"

"Uhm, I don't know. Not too much."

"Well, I think they're overfiltered, you know?"

"Right. Overfiltered."

"You don't get that much tobacco taste."

"True. True."

"But we might as well smoke them. They're free."

Sure thing, thought Frankie, might as well. If they're free.

Laurel held her cup in her right hand, along with the cigarette. Her left hand was abandoned to her lap. The cigarette stuck out prominently from the tips of her fingers; the cup was suspended beneath it by the pressure of her thumb and her cigarette fingers. The smoke rose in a wispy column toward the trees.

She raised her elegantly cluttered hand in the traditional sign of cheer. "To you, Frankie. I'm so very glad that it's over with."

Frankie smiled. "To me."

"And now—to us."

"Right. To us."

The booze and the dry cigarette mixed energetically, spurring them to a restless activity. Like so much excess energy, it manifested itself in speech.

"Laurel."

"Frankie."

"Good stuff, huh?"

"Good stuff. Are you a little high?"

"Maybe a little. You?"

"Maybe a little."

They drank again, to fill up the silence. Frankie stubbed out his cigarette; Laurel's was barely half burned.

"So, look"—he raised his cup—"where's the celebration? We're supposed to be celebrating, right?"

"Right."

"Okay."

He waited. Now what?

"To us," she volunteered.

"To us."

They lapsed again into silence. Frankie was almost uncomfortable when Laurel entered abruptly.

"Frankie?"

"Yeah?"

"Tell me something."

"What?"

"What do you think you'll do when you get out of school?"

"I don't know. Go to college, I guess."

"You will?"

"Sure."

"What are you going to take?"

"I don't know."

"You'll probably play basketball, anyway, huh?"

"I guess I will. If I can."

"If you can? What do you mean, if you can? Of course you will."

"Well, we'll see. I don't know."

"Come on, don't be so modest. Don't forget, I know that you were all-city this year. And you still have a year to go."

"So?"

"So you'll get better."

Frankie laughed. "It doesn't always work that way."

"I bet it does most of the time."

He shrugged.

Laurel took a breath and continued, "I still remember the day we walked into Lopez. I think I saw you right away."

"You did?"

"Sure I did. And you know what?"

"What?"

"Just about the first thing I heard in there was that you were all-city, the very first thing, just after you left for your game. Everybody else knows how good you are, how come you don't?"

Jesus, Frankie thought, was that true? "What am I, a celebrity?"

Laurel laughed. "Sure you are. You're a star."

A star, oh God. They both laughed, the star and his girl friend.

"How would you like to be a starlet?" he asked her, but she was being serious through her laughter.

"No, really. I don't think you give yourself enough credit."

"Of course I do."

"No you don't, Frankie. Or else you wouldn't talk so depressingly about yourself."

"I'm not depressed."

"You sound it."

"Just because I don't come on like Joe All-Star or something? That doesn't mean anything, Laurel. I know what I can do."

"You do?"

"Sure. I'm realistic."

"Okay, then what's all that garbage about 'maybe' making the team, or 'maybe' playing basketball in college?"

"Laurel, listen, that's just being realistic, that's all."

"That's not being realistic, that's being gloomy. All you have to do is try, you'll do it."

"There's more to it than that."

"If you try hard enough, if you really push for it, you'll make it."

Frankie shook his head. "Oh, I don't know."

"Everybody knows you can do it but you."

"Everybody? Who's everybody?"

"Everybody. I can tell by the way they talk that they think you'll make it. Just by the way they talk about it."

Frankie shrugged. Laurel paused and brought the subject to even greater heights. "You could even make it to the pros."

"The pros? Laurel, come on, I'm not even big enough to string the baskets."

But she was firm. "You've got to try. You've just got to set your sights on it and try. How will you ever know for sure if you don't?"

Well, that's true enough, he thought. You'll never know if you don't try. That sounded reasonable. "We'll see, Laurel, we'll see."

Pretty soon she'd have him filling in for Doctor J at the foul line in a crucial situation. The crowd yelling and shouting from the rafters. O'DAY! O'DAY! O'DAY! Then, while twenty thousand watched in person, and twenty million on TV, he'd blow the shot. Choke. Frankie chuckled at the thought. Laurel responded, with a wide smile, and they stared at each other once again. He leaned over and kissed her. "We'll see."

"Sure. We'll see."

"How about a refill?" he asked, leaning back for the bags.

"Why not?"

She drained the cup of its contents and handed it over to Frankie. He set everything up and began his measuring and pouring, but he found it a little more difficult to handle this time, as if someone had moved something and he had to rearrange things to get them back in order. When he finished with the vodka and was slopping in the unmeasured quantity of orange juice, he recovered enough to speak. "What about you?"

"What about me?"

"Yeah, what about you? What are you going to do?"

"You mean, after high school?"

"After high school."

"Oh, go to college. Maybe USC, but I don't really know."

"Oh."

"I think I'll major in education."

"You want to be a teacher?"

"I think so, yeah. In the early grades."

"Oh."

Frankie was surprised by the length to which her plans had been made. Right through college out into the world. He was also taken aback by the unforeseen specificity: USC, teaching grade school, and all that. It surprised him and it also made him retreat, as if there were no part for him in such plans. He was very quiet then, feeling suddenly numb inside, and not entirely from the vodka. It was something else which he'd been dreading, and which he'd managed to forget, but which now rose to meet him like the ghost of an old embarrassment.

"Ah—Laurel?"

"Yes?"

"Uhm—tell me, what's the story on this Lake Tahoe thing?"

"Lake Tahoe thing?"

"Yeah. You know. Your cottage."

"Oh." She understood and was silent.

Frankie asked, "When are you supposed to go?"

She spoke softly, as if she were hesitant to release

the information. "Next week. Or the week after, I forget."

"Wow," Frankie said, lowering his own voice to meet hers. "It's so soon."

"Yeah."

"Hey, can you get out of it?"

"Can I get out of it?"

"Yeah, you know, can you get out of going up?"

"I don't know."

He wondered if she had even considered the idea of getting out of it, or of putting it off, or anything along those lines. What if she hadn't even thought about it? Maybe she hadn't the slightest intention of getting out of it. After all, she had said that she was crazy about the place.

They drank in silence and he wondered what she was thinking. The cars plowed by, in a kind of stroboscopic progression, on the other side of the trees. When he snuck a look at Laurel, her face was so close to his shoulder, he knew she was thinking and could only hope that she'd say something to bring him back, to save him.

She said nothing, but finally she sighed and put her left hand on the cap of his knee, squeezing it gently and reassuringly. He placed his own hand on top of hers and squeezed.

"It's just . . ." He stopped and gathered his thoughts. "It's just that I'd be very sorry to see you go."

She looked up at him and smiled, her eyes thick and shining, almost as if she were going to cry. "I know," she whispered.

"And I'd much rather have you stay."

She nodded.

"So—can you?"

He barely spoke this last entreaty. It made the silence that followed all the heavier. He could hear something new, a ringing sensation in his ears that hadn't been perceptible before. And the distant breath of the traffic.

Her head collapsed on his shoulder and she began to weep. He rushed to put his arm around her and to comfort her.

"Laurel, hey, what's the matter?"

She continued crying but didn't speak.

"Laurel, hey, come on."

He rocked her with the strength of his arm, back and forth, surprised at the instinctive ease with which his action came. "Don't cry."

"I know. I can't help it," she said, through the dishevelment of her tears.

"Don't cry."

And he kept rocking her, back and forth, like something sweet and regular, back and forth, a dance, an embrace, something soothing for her to come down to. Something easy.

He whispered, "Don't cry."

"Okay."

"I'm sorry if . . ."

She shook her head against his shoulder. "It wasn't anything you said, Frankie, it was just . . ."

"Just what?"

"Oh—I don't know. Just me, that's all."

"It's okay."

"Just everything coming on at once, you know?"

"I know."

"I mean, I really want to stay, like, if I could, you know?"

"I know."

"But I don't know how I can, and . . ."

Her voice was becoming stronger and more collected as it went along. The brief outburst of tears was on the wane, but there was something human and defenseless which it had left behind.

"I know, Laurel. I just wish you could, that's all."

"Me, too."

She looked up, with her miraculous eyes a shower of light in the darkness. Frankie squeezed her shoulders and tried to tell her, "I really just—just wish you could."

"Well, let's see."

"Let's see what?"

"Well, maybe there's a possibility."

"There is?"

"Just an outside one."

"I'll take it." He said it quickly, almost clowning for the first time since she'd begun crying.

"It's just an outside chance," she repeated, slowly, as if calculating some last-minute amendment to her secret plan. "Maybe I can do it."

"Maybe you can do it?"

"Sure, maybe. I'll just see if I can stay at home during the week, like Daddy, and go up on weekends."

"That wouldn't be too bad, would it?"

"No, and it's possible he'll agree, I don't know. He's so stubborn when he makes up his mind. Stubborn as a bull."

"An ass."

"What?"

"Stubborn as an ass, you know? A donkey."

"Oh, whatever."

Laurel was getting a little drunk. Her words came forth with unusual inflections. Of course Frankie was getting a little drunk, too, so the oddity of a few slurs here and there didn't bother him much at all. Still, he noticed that she had trouble with the word stubborn, pronouncing it shtubbin, which was unlike her.

She did it again—"He's so shtubbin"—and this time Frankie noticed a tone of long-suffering endearment in her voice, like a mother speaking of her tow-headed, recalcitrant child.

"Just try, Laurel. Who knows? It might be no problem at all."

"No problem at all. Who knows?"

Her voice slid back toward the tears then, pleading, "I just hope I can do it, Frankie, I just hope I can."

"It's okay, Laurel, just give it a try."

"I guess so."

She wiped her eyes with her sleeve, bravely, as if she were determined to break from her melancholy as soon as possible. She bravely took another slug of the screwdriver and spoke. "I'm sorry about the crying. I don't know what came over me."

"It's okay."

"It's just that I'm not a person who's always bursting into tears, you know? You can always count on that. No tears."

Frankie squeezed her. "Don't worry about it."

"I won't. It's just I felt so—so hopeless or something all of a sudden. So—squeezed."

"It's okay."

"I know. It's over now. An' don't worry, this is a girl who doesn't break down and cry at the drop of a hat."

"I know that."

"Well, I just wanted you to know."

"I know."

"Do you ever cry, Frankie?"

"Me? I don't know. Maybe sometimes."

"When?"

"I don't know. Uh. Not too much."

"When was the last time?"

"Oh, I don't remember, Laurel, it's not important. I don't know."

She was quiet, so he felt compelled to elaborate. "Oh, well, it might have been—uh—"

He didn't remember. He couldn't remember the last time he'd cried. It must have been closer than the bruised, salty tears of his childhood, remembered through a kind of academic mist of tears. It must have been more recently than that. But he couldn't remember.

Laurel interrupted his searching. "Doesn't anything hurt you?"

"Of course it does. Lots of things hurt me. Every-

thing hurts me. All the time things hurt me. I—I just
don't seem to cry about them too much lately."
"You don't?"
"No. Not lately. I don't know. Sometimes I think
that if we let ourselves start crying, we'd end up crying
all the time. What good would that do?"
"Not much. Not much."
Silence followed then. Frankie thought of nothing;
his mind was in unmanageable disarray, as if all his
thoughts had suddenly run out on him. Laurel made her
statement then.
"Frankie, you know you ought to be a poet."
She spoke softly, happily, but with unswerving
conviction in her voice. Frankie didn't answer. Her
innocent statement brought dozens of scenes to his
mind. He saw the first careful slogans he'd lettered on
the Loyola walls. (A poet, she said.) He also saw the one
he'd done after his last "poetry" night with Laurel.

> Cast a cold eye
> On life on death
> Horseman pass by
> —the shadow

(A poet was what he *ought* to be. That's what he *ought*
to be.)
He might be able to talk to her of these things, all
scattered and kind of tawdry in their way, but it was just
so hard to begin. Someday it would be good, he thought,
to just confess everything to her, out with it all, whatever there was in there to be evicted. He could start with
grammar school, or even earlier, childhood, and it
might be good to just dump the whole story on her, just

to see what she'd say. It was possible that he could make a small beginning tonight, but he couldn't quite think of the right words to introduce such a conversation.

Excuse me, Miss, get comfortable, will you, while I tell you my life story.

No, that wouldn't do.

It would be better if it came up gradually, later on. Let it come out naturally. Let everything they would do together come naturally.

For all of Frankie's internal debate, he said nothing. Instead it was Laurel who spoke, singing her version of T. S. Eliot.

> *"In the room the women come and go*
> *Singing of Michelangelo."*

She kept singing it, in her whisper voice, and the effect was so entrancing that it seemed to Frankie that this must have been the way the poem had been written.

> *"In the room the women come and go*
> *Singing of Michelangelo."*

All the legions of women, in waves of colorful dresses and costumes, flowing through the art gallery singing about Michelangelo. Laurel's sweet soft voice would be lost in such a throng, but it would add its own small strength to the trembling chorus.

> *"In the room the women come and go*
> *Singing of Michelangelo."*

She stopped singing and cleared her throat.
"Frankie?"
"What?"

"I was juss thinking. You know what?"

"What?" It was amazing how her voice had changed, had lost definition somehow, as if she were talking through a mouth that had been shot full of novocaine. It was cute, but only because it was Laurel.

"You know what?"

He chuckled. "What?"

"Well—you won't believe this."

"I won't believe what?"

"You'll never believe it." She giggled, secretly.

"Laurel, I'll never believe what?"

"Well. 'Member a long, long time ago, when we were both about six'r seven'r so?"

"Yeah?"

"Well—I already decided, even then, that I wanted to come to Sanfrasisco."

"Sanfrasisco?" He laughed.

"San-fra-sisco." That was the best she could do.

"Sanfrasisco."

"I was in Corpus Christi then an' I wanted to run away to Sanfrasisco."

"You did?"

"You bet I did. Course I never acshally did, but I wanted to."

"How come?"

"Well, you know, I kepp seein' Sanfrasisco on TV and everything, and everybody seemed so beautiful, you know? Everybody was always smiling an' the hills all had flowers all over them. Seemed like heaven'r something, you know?"

"Yeah, well, it's not heaven, I don't think."

"What about you? You ever wanna run away to Sanfrasisco when you were six'r seven'r so?"

"How could I? I was already here."

"Oh, yeah. Right."

Frankie leaned back against the tree. He sipped from the remnants of his drink and remembered.

"I know what you mean, though, and I'm trying to think if I ever had the feeling that San Francisco was a special place when I was growing up. I really don't think I did. It was just the place where I happened to be, that's all. You know what I mean?"

Laurel uttered a faint sound which indicated that she understood. Frankie was numb in his lips but he felt like talking. He spoke slowly and thoughtfully; there was no hurry.

"I can think of one time, one time when I was small and I remember how everyone talked about how great San Francisco was. It was pretty strange, really. You're going to think I was a strange little kid, but it wasn't me as much as it was the situation.

"Anyway, it was at a reception of some sort they were giving at the St. Francis. A cocktail party or something. It was given in honor of this North Beach poet—I don't even remember the guy's name—but he'd just had his first book published in hardcover. It was a big deal.

"The only reason I was there was thanks to my baby-sitter, who cancelled at the last minute with some trumped-up excuse or another. I think her rosebush died or something.

"So, there I was, the only kid in the place, and

there was everyone else, swilling martinis and talking about the famous 'literary life' of San Francisco. I didn't even know what that meant, but I figured it was important, the way they carried on about it.

"I felt kind of embarrassed when my mother took me around and introduced me to everybody. They all said I was cute and they all asked me did I want to be a famous San Francisco poet when I grew up? Naturally I said yes, and everyone laughed. I couldn't figure out what was so funny. The way I saw it, I was giving them the answer they were looking for, and every time I did they laughed their asses off. I couldn't figure that out.

"Finally they took me to meet the famous North Beach poet. I can remember him as if it were yesterday. He looked like a bunch of rags tossed over a chair, a bunch of rags with a giant curly beard on top.

"Worst of all, he smelled *terrible.* He stunk. I couldn't get away from him fast enough. He wanted to put his arms around me, this famous poet, and I just yelled something about having to go to the bathroom and I took off.

"Boy, was I glad to get away from him.

"Funny thing was, I figured I was out of danger when I stormed into the bathroom, and shut the door behind me, when what should I find in there but this other guy, on his hands and knees, *talking* to the toilet. Carrying on a conversation. Saying things like, 'They don't understand me. Only you understand me.'

"I was frozen to the spot. Finally this great friend of toilets left off his conversation and turned to look at me. And that's what really freaked me out. His eyes were wild; they looked like pinwheels in his head. Totally gonzo.

"Thinking back, I can see that he was probably on some kind of weirdo mind drug, but back then the only thing that made sense was that he was a werewolf or something. Ate little boys for breakfast.

"So I raced out of there even faster than I'd raced in. My mother could see there was something wrong and she hustled me right out of there and out to the car.

"I calmed down in the car on the way home and I can remember my mother asking me what was wrong and the only thing I could tell her was that I hated poets. I wonder if she ever really understood.

"It's funny now. . . ."

Laurel had said with such conviction that he should be a poet. He'd been surprisingly pleased when she'd said it. He thought he'd ask her about it. He knew also that it would necessarily lead them on to the subject of his walls.

It was with a touch of nervousness, then, that he took one large swallow of his drink and asked, "Laurel?"

Laurel didn't move.

"Laurel?"

She grunted.

"Laurel, you okay?"

She grunted again. Frankie bent his head forward to look at her. Her eyes were closed and her mouth was open.

"Laurel?"

"Wha?"

"Laurel, you okay?"

"Baffroom."

"What?"

"Baffroom. Wanna go baffroom."

Oh, hell, he thought, she's really bombed.

"Okay, here, I'll help you up."

He got her on her feet and she seemed to benefit from the effort. Her eyes opened and blinked themselves into shape as she steadied herself with her hand against the tree.

"You okay, Laurel?"

"Yup, 'm fine. 'M fine."

"You still have to go to the bathroom?"

"Yeah. Juss let me go rounn the corner. Be right back."

"You sure you're okay?"

"Okay. Okay."

She guided herself past the tree and down the path and into the bushes between the path and the road. Frankie waited. As long as she stayed on her feet and didn't drink anymore, she would probably be all right.

It hit her so quickly. One minute she was as lucid as a pane of glass, the next she was down for the count. One thing was in his favor: At least her breath wouldn't smell when he brought her home.

He soon became concerned when he could hear no sound or movement from the direction in which she'd disappeared. He waited as long as he could, a respectable time, before setting off to find her. She might be in trouble.

He walked slowly, listening for some fragile sound

through the rhythmic pounding of the blood in his head. But the only sound he heard was the crackle of his own footsteps over the dark dry ground.

When he had walked all the way to the edge of the park without spotting her, his imagination sprang instantly into action, creating all sorts of disasters, from concussion to rape. He squinted in the artificial light and searched the street for some sign of her. There was none. There was only the traffic.

Turning quickly, he launched himself back into the woods. Coming now from this direction, with the pale streetlight at his back, he saw her right away. She was sitting, with her back against a tree, and her legs spread in the shape of a diamond, held at the bottom by her freshly bleached jeans, fallen to her ankles, and at the top by the dark, soft object of Frankie's desire. Her knees were thrown carelessly out, in a position of graceless, all-forgiving acceptance, and the sight made Frankie's heart ache.

He was suddenly very, very sorry.

"Laurel, honey, sweetheart, sweetheart, oh, no. Here, let me help you, let me help you, let me help you— there—that's it—pull them up—you do it—that's it. Oh, baby, baby, don't worry, don't worry, I'll take care of you—here, let me help you—there—I'll take care of you, Frankie won't let you down, Frankie'll take care of you."

Anyone who saw them walking home could only have thought that they were the most sublime of lovers, walking as one being, wedded by emotion to each other. In fact, Laurel was half asleep the whole way and

Frankie held her as much from fear as from devotion. But he did love her, now more than ever, and there was that weight of sorrow in his heart to prove it.

When they got to her house Frankie was relieved to see that all was dark inside. He helped her up the stairs and they paused before the big Spanish door.

"Have you got your key?"

With her eyes closed, she reached into her jacket pocket and presented him with the key. He opened the door and pushed it gently inward. Laurel took the key, marched into the house, and slammed the door behind her. Frankie heard the heavy *clunk* of the lock mechanism as the door stopped just inches short of his head.

The next sound he heard was the dull thumping sound of a body descending rapidly toward a peaceful, unconscious heap on the Spanish entranceway floor.

PART

The next week was a particularly desolate one for Frankie. It began immediately, on Sunday morning. The phone rang in the quiet house.

"Frankie?"

"Yeah."

"It's Pauline."

"Oh, hi, Pauline."

"Hi."

She waited, expecting, no doubt, that he would say something. When he didn't, she volunteered the information.

"Things don't look too good, Frankie."

"They don't?"

"Nope."

"What do you mean?"

Pauline sighed, a great rush of vacant sound through the telephone receiver, and let it all out.

"It's pretty bad, Frankie, pretty bad. You shouldn't have left her like that."

"I couldn't help it."

"Yeah, well, I think she feels really embarrassed about the whole thing."

"Embarrassed?"

"Yeah. Her father found her like that in the morning."

"Oh."

The telephone line crackled and yielded to the silence. Distant, phantom conversations surfaced and sank somewhere in the ocean of electronic synapses which the telephone touched. Frankie listened to their faint jabbering and once again tried to make some sense of their voices but could not. They were just disembodied, busy souls, clucking like so many chickens on the other side of the murky, telephonic darkness.

Pauline's voice fairly boomed forth. "Well, I gotta get going."

"Wait," said Frankie, "I don't understand. What's going to happen to her?"

"Oh, I don't know. She'll be in the doghouse for a while, that's for sure."

"How long?"

"Oh, a while. And you'll be off limits for quite a while, too."

"Me? How come?"

"What do you mean, how come? You're the one who got her into all this, aren't you?"

"No. I mean—not on my own."

Pauline made a clucking sound with her tongue. "Who helped you?"

"Who helped me? Laurel helped me. You know?"

"Oh, come on, Frankie."

"No, I mean—why is it all my fault?"

"Frankie, come on. Who else is there to blame?"

Beautiful. Frankie felt a knot of frustration beginning to form at the top of his stomach. It would be there, in greater or lesser degree, throughout the week.

"Pauline, tell her to call me, will you? If she can?"

"Well, she's not supposed to. . . ."

"Please, just tell her to try."

"Well—I can't promise anything, Frankie."

"Just ask her to try."

"Okay. I'll ask her to try."

Thus began the waiting.

He spent all day Sunday knocking restlessly about the house. He and his father watched the Giants game in relative silence. The game was a bore and he spent most of his time going to the refrigerator, or to the bathroom, or even just to the window to look out.

Sometimes he walked by the phone and looked at it ruefully before continuing on into the living room. It was a stupid, miserable afternoon.

He and his mother ate dinner at about four o'clock, while his father slept. His father awoke and ate later, around six-thirty. Frankie went to his room and read a book about bees taking over the world.

He went over to the Prayerbook court on Monday morning, passing quickly by Lopez on the way. Neither Laurel nor Pauline was anywhere to be seen. He hadn't expected to see them.

When he got to the court, only Number 44 was there, throwing up mechanical set shots from about five feet out. They exchanged a wordless greeting and began a quick game of one-on-one. The kid was so quick that the game soon got the best of Frankie, trying to keep up with him. It was a challenge.

Frankie was quick, himself, especially for his size. He had about eight inches on 44, but the kid made up in speed what he lacked in size. It was almost a standoff. Number 44 beat him for a couple of lay-ups, but not too many. And he stood his ground on defense and forced Frankie to take a lot of outside shots, but even when he missed, Frankie could usually get over him to grab the rebound. The rebounds he could put up from in close. What kept 44 in the game was his lightning-quick outside shot. Frankie would have to guard against the drive and, whenever he overcommitted himself, 44 would stop on a dime and be up in the air before Frankie could even brace himself to defend against the jump shot. His shot was accurate; it had to be. Frankie allowed him no second chances.

When they had exhausted themselves sufficiently at this, and still no others came to join their game, they rested together at the side of the court. Out of breath, they could do nothing with each other but smile and blow out hot, wet drafts of air into the vacuum.

Frankie paced in circles, to get his legs back, and he stared up at the giant dark silhouette of the stone Prayerbook Cross against the pale blue sky. It made him think of Laurel.

They were rested by then, and ready to return to the court, but no one else had come, and Frankie wasn't really interested in playing. If he had bothered to pin it down, he would probably have realized that what he wanted to do was to go home and get a call from Laurel, explaining everything. As it happened, he only realized that he wanted to go home. The call would have to come of its own accord.

"I'm gonna split, man," he said. "Catch you later."

Number 44 smiled and nodded, heading back for the court. Frankie walked away. When he looked back once, over his shoulder, he saw 44 back at the basket, tossing up mechanical set shots from about five feet out.

There was no call on Monday, no call on Monday night. On Tuesday he walked by her house, but everything inside was dark and mysterious. There was nothing he could do but continue walking. He stopped by

Lopez, but she wasn't there and there was no one there he wanted to talk to.

By this time he was alternately loving her and missing her and hating her and despairing of her soul and her character. He didn't know what to think. He waited.

The phone didn't ring.

He wondered what in the world she was thinking about.

He even thought that she might have found someone else. Someone else to bless with her eyes.

And the phone didn't ring.

He thought of her father and of how much she loved him. How much she was scared of him. How much he represented everything Frankie could never get close to, and of how he represented everything Laurel was fated to achieve.

He felt—abandoned.

And the phone did not ring.

On Tuesday night, when he couldn't stand it anymore, Frankie went out after supper and down to Lopez. Not that he thought he'd find Laurel there, in fact he supposed he wouldn't, but it was an outlet for his energy, an action he felt competent to perform.

There was no one at Lopez but Bob Gatz, who had tucked himself into the first booth and was drinking a small glass of orange juice.

"Frankie, how ya doing?"

"Good, Bob, you?"

"Good."

Frankie looked around once, pointlessly, and sat down.

"Quiet tonight."

"Yup."

He asked Mr. Lopez for a coffee regular and tried to relax.

"I don't know, Bob, I don't know. How are things going?"

"Oh, pretty good," he said, lifting the tiny juice glass with a movement of his entire beefy arm, stiff and nearly useless for anything but football.

"That's good. You still working out?"

"Oh, yeah. Every day, every day."

"Hard work, huh?"

Bob screwed his face into a grimace. "You bet. But it's worth it."

Frankie accepted his coffee and stirred it. "It must get pretty hot now under those pads."

"Oh, yeah. Oh, yeah. But it peels any extra fat you might have right off the bone."

"I'm sure it does."

"Oh, yeah."

They paused to lift their drinks to their mouths. Frankie tasted the coffee sweet and thick around his tongue. He thought how nice a cigarette would taste, but he didn't have any. Bob didn't smoke.

To keep the conversation going, he finally asked him, "You got any feelers yet from the colleges?"

"Couple."

"Anyplace special?"

"Yeah. Ohio State."

Frankie almost tipped over his cup. "Ohio State? You shitting me?"

"No. I got a letter from the coach inviting me to come out this fall."

"Hey, Bob, man, that's great. Ohio State. Too much. Hey, well, congratulations."

"Thanks," he said, with genuine modesty, "but that's what I've been working toward, that's what I've been doing all this for."

"Wow, Ohio State."

Frankie could hardly believe it. He felt good about it, though, he felt good for Bob. There was no jealousy at all, just a kind of warm feeling that came from looking at the wide glow which emanated from Bob's face. He had certainly worked for it.

"It's really something, Frankie, I'll tell you. It really makes you feel good. Hell, I might not even get an offer, you know? Or I might not make the team? But whatever happens, that I made it this far seems to make it all worthwhile."

Frankie thought how Bob's father must feel, after all his tampering with his son's body to achieve a goal such as this. It probably convinced him that he had been successful. It probably convinced him that he had done the right thing by his son, and by himself. There was something unpoetic and disturbing about that.

But as far as Bob was concerned, there could only be further joy, since he had proven to his father so dramatically his own worth. It had been worth his father's time, he would think, because he'd shown him he could do it, he could come up to those standards. It made no difference that the standards were all fucked up, it only counted that you met them.

Frankie looked over at Bob and smiled. He loved him, all of a sudden. He felt like squeezing his lumpy hand and wishing him luck and going through all those emotional dances that people sometimes give themselves up to. He also felt sad for what he understood would be a future comedown for Bob, when his thin, tendentious balloon would be suddenly and without warning burst and he would fly around the room spitting dreams and missed opportunities out behind him.

But who knows? He might even make it.

"Bob, man, good luck, I mean it."

"Thanks, Frankie."

"Hey, look, I've got to get going. Take it easy, okay?"

"Yeah, Frankie, you, too. See you around."

"Right. See you around."

He met Billy Lyons outside on the sidewalk.

"Frankie. How ya doing?"

"Billy. Okay."

"Hey, man, come here a second, will you? I got something I wanna talk to you about."

"What is it?"

"Well, it's a gag, you know?"

"Yeah, sure thing, Billy, let me know how it comes out."

"What do you mean, how it comes out?"

"Jesus, I'm still trying to get over the last one, you know?" Frankie smiled and shook his head. He was trying his best to appear graceful and yet manage to extricate himself from whatever it was Billy had coming.

"Yeah, but that was different," Billy said. "We didn't *plan* that one and besides, it was a little crazy to begin with."

"Crazy? You sure?"

"A little."

Frankie shook his head again. A little. He tried to change the subject. "How's your brother?"

"Sonny? He's okay. He's out, you know. Don't worry about Sonny, he'll be okay. He told me they don't really have a case on him. He'll get off."

"He will?"

"Sure, man, don't worry about old Sonny."

That was truly the last thing Frankie would do, worry about old Sonny.

"But, look, man," said Billy, "I want to lay something else on you now. It'll be dynamite."

Sure. Explode in their faces. "I don't think so, Billy."

"Ah, come on. You haven't even heard me out yet. You don't even know what it's about."

"I like it that way. A real surprise."

"Frankie, man, come on. You're gonna like this one."

"Yeah, well, I don't know."

"Just listen. You know Kramer, Ralphie Kramer? His father owns Kramer Konstruction down in Burlingame?"

Frankie knew him, vaguely.

"Well, his old man's out of town, I think he's in

Peru or someplace, and Ralphie's been doing a lot of work for him. Taking care of the trucks and shit like that.

"Well, anyway, Ralphie's come up with a plan. He's got a whole truckload of fairly rough gravel and he's got that mixed with some sand and some portland cement. And right now it's all just sittin' there, waiting to do something. So what we're trying to figure is what to do with it.

"Ralphie's idea was to dump it on somebody's car during the night and have it harden so that when the poor bastard comes out in the morning his car's permanently buried under a big pile of concrete. Myself, I thought that was a little extreme. I figured that to dump it on someone's lawn would be just as good and not quite so nasty, you know what I mean?"

Frankie knew. He thought about dumping it on Laurel's lawn, but that would probably do very little to win back her father's affection.

Win back her father's affection? The whole idea was absolutely incredible. He felt like an insurance man or something.

Billy closed his mouth and shook his head. He must have been following his own train of thought. He looked back up and spoke. "But even that really isn't so hot, you know, man? There's got to be some better idea. Like, you know, dump it in the middle of Market Street or something."

Great idea.

Frankie shook his head. "I don't know where to dump it."

"Come on, man, think. We've got to come up with something soon or else it'll rain and all that cement will stick to the truck. Ralphie's old man'll have his ass."

"Maybe you should dump it on the mayor's lawn?"

"Nah, I don't think so. I'm not into that political shit, you know? Besides, there's so much security around politicians nowadays you can't get near them. Armed guards with orders to shoot on sight."

"Okay, what about North Beach? You could try to dump it on Carol Doda."

"Far out. Good idea, but it sounds like it'd be tough to pull off."

"How about Telegraph Hill?"

"Where? On the statue?"

"I don't know. There, or else just on the hill. How about right at the entrance there, where the road narrows. You could cover the whole thing."

"Right, right." Billy was thinking. "Right, I see it. Incredible. The whole mess right there, sealing them off."

"Sealing who off?"

"The lovers, man, the crazy lovers on lover's lane. All the Mister Clean college types with their weekend girl friends. There they are up there every Friday night, with Daddy's car, trying to get a little head from some local debutante. Or maybe it's Mary Jane from Bryn Mawr back for the summer letting herself go a bit, after a proper movie and a few drinks, and getting planked by some sport in a Jaguar. You know the scene."

Frankie knew the scene. It made him think of Laurel and wince.

"So, dig it, Frankie, you hit it right on the head. We wait 'til late Friday night, when old Johnnie and Janie are up there getting it on (they won't even hear us), and just before they have to get Daddy's car home—say, quarter of twelve—we dump it on 'em. Seal the fuckers in there. Ha ha, ha HA! I'd like to see 'em explain that one to Daddy."

"Or to the road people, for that matter," said Frankie.

"Right on, right on. I hope they're all getting their rocks off just as we dump our load."

Frankie laughed. Billy's crazy enthusiasm was enough to infect anyone. "Maybe they won't be able to dig them out 'til morning."

"Right on," said Billy, "right on. They'll have to get a bulldozer." He broke out laughing again. "Can't you just see the looks on their faces, these slick Harvard hard-ons, after they've made their conquest, and the little curly-haired girl is still blushing and rearranging her clothes, and this suave bastard backs his MG out of the space, and then drives smack into a pile of cement in the roadway?"

They both laughed as if someone were tickling them.

"Jesus."

Frankie kept laughing, right along with Billy, until his sides ached and wet tears welled in his eyes.

Billy tried to continue talking. "And—and—and—they'll be stuck there all night, in the MG, John and Jane, so when they get home in the morning everyone'll think they've been balling even if they haven't."

"Yeah, and they'll probably all get pregnant, 'cause they can't get home to shoot up that foam or whatever it is."

"A baby boom."

"Like The Great Blackout."

"And all thanks to you, Frankie, beautiful."

"Yeah, right."

"Hey, look, I'll get back to you, Frankie. First I gotta talk to Ralphie about it." Billy was already restless, drifting away, anxious to get the plan into action.

"Okay. Catch you later, Billy."

"Yeah. I hope it doesn't rain before Friday night."

"Right."

After Billy had left, Frankie tried to recreate in his mind the scenes of hilarity which he'd experienced the moment before, but he couldn't quite remember. All he could see was a dump truck spilling out a large gray mound of concrete on a strip of narrow blacktop. After that there was nothing.

When he awakened on Wednesday morning, Frankie found that his restless vigilance had been replaced by a numb acceptance. Perhaps it was just the morning. Perhaps it was because she didn't call and it is not in the interest of human resilience to pursue a fleeing phantom for too long. It might become a habit.

But numbness, too, can be habitual, and Frankie had no way of knowing how the safe walls of his retreat could so easily close, like a flower in the cool night, and imprison him. He knew only that he had to get out.

He went by Lopez again, without seeing Laurel or

Pauline, and he resisted a turn to the Prayerbook court to head downtown instead.

The creaking bus, which had been so sparsely settled when he boarded, began to fill as they approached their Market Street destination. All the people who entered were, like Frankie, the unintegrated elements of society. They were the drifters; the nonworkers; the old men and the young boys; the cowled old ladies with their shopping bags filled with rags; the middle-aged blacks, long out of work and used to it, staring like statues from their sad, unshaven faces; the bored housewives going out to look in shop windows and to dream of some secret fling they might someday encounter; and two nuns, sitting quietly together and smiling, like one element only, and unaware of its own estrangement. Frankie sat in the back like a spy.

They all got off at the same stop downtown and scattered, mixing as well as they could with the messenger boys and businessmen who circulated like a stream of busy, fatal leukocytes through the heart of the downtown streets. Frankie watched and wandered.

He wandered through the financial district and over past Gump's Store down to Union Square, where the tourists came and waited for the Powell Street cable car. He walked quickly past I. Magnin and Macy's, where the streets were swollen with shopping bags and with fresh beige boxes, tied with new white string and hanging from copper handles. He turned and walked through the Tenderloin, with its old and unsavory reputation. In the blanching sunlight it only looked old.

When he was back to Market Street he turned and

headed downtown, toward the ferry building, whose tower peeked above the jagged rooftops toward the sky. The walk had relaxed him, and he felt good enough to print his epitaph on the window of the bombed-out edifice which might once have been the JC Penney store.

> When I am dead
> I hope it may be said
> His house was scarlet
> But his walls were read
> —the shadow

It made him feel infinitely better. None of the hollow, vacant-eyed passersby took any notice of him, but he knew there would be others who would see it later. They'd wonder who this Shadow was. They might be scared of him, or they might project all sorts of private fascinations onto his unknown person, but they would notice. That, he guessed, was what The Shadow was all about.

Frankie smiled and went about his wandering.

He stopped by a newsstand that looked like a baby cable car and perused the day's selection. Some magazines like *Time* and *Newsweek*, the usual potpourri of underground rags with headlines like

PIGS BUST PEOPLE ON THE HEAD AT UC RALLY

The *Examiner* had a headline and a story on the RFK assassination. He read it with interest.

What kind of world are we running nowadays anyway?

The story claimed that new evidence had surfaced proving that Sirhan Sirhan could not have killed Bobby Kennedy. Beautiful. They had the whole thing on film practically, and they grabbed Sirhan on the spot, with the gun, fifty people saw him, or said they did, just so that new evidence could be uncovered years later that proved it couldn't be him. What kind of logic is that? Frankie could not remember the JFK assassination; he'd seen the picture of Oswald being killed: one man lunging suddenly from a crowd and the other collapsing suddenly into his stomach, as if to chase the fatal bullet. But even that series of events was far from settled, after all this time. And the King murder, what was the story on that one?

But Sirhan Sirhan? He practically did it onstage, for God's sake.

There was just nothing in the world you could count on, nothing was a certainty anymore. In the old days, when someone killed someone, somebody caught them and they had a trial and were executed, or put in jail, or whatever. That was it. It might not have been fair always, but at least it was something you could count on.

Nowadays you couldn't count on anything.

Frankie wandered downtown in a renewed daze. When he'd reached the withered end of Market Street, in the no-man's-land near the Embarcadero, he found a wall of newly minted plywood upon which he could vent his spleen.

178 • Walls

Flash!
Sirhan Sirhan was the real murderer
of Lee Harvey Oswald—
Jack Ruby was a corporate puppet
                                        —the shadow

It looked so authoritative on the fresh new plywood that Frankie almost believed it himself. After he'd
read it over a few times, he began to think, Why not?
Perhaps the whole idea wasn't so bizarre after all. No
more so than anything else.

A mindless, grumbling sound came from behind
the plywood and attracted his attention. He peeked
through the crack where the nearest slab of plywood
joined his own and saw that they were digging a gigantic hole in the earth. Huge, grunting machines
carved out tons of black dirt and loaded it on the
patient backs of dwarfed, puffing dump trucks. Each
of these rolled obligingly away from the site, to de-
posit its dark cargo in some unnamed and desolate
region, where it would await, perhaps, yet another
transport.

The sign said Kramer Konstruction Kompany. It
made him think that all this might even connect somehow, it might all be related, but there was just no way
to figure it all out. It was a numb, disheartening realiza-
tion, something like defeat. And the giant thoughtless
earthmovers struggled on.

The volume of rumbling, herky-jerky activity
made him suddenly tired. The late afternoon sun had
grown harsh and derisive with the day. He turned and

walked slowly back to Market Street, where he caught
the N Judah heading home.

No calls during supper. Frankie found himself
falling into old, preternatural modes of behavior.
At precisely 6:30 P.M., he knew she would call, he
knew she stood in the vicinity of her phone, with her
hand and mind poised to call him, and still she
didn't call.

He waited until eight. The telepathic feeling vanished then, as if it had calmly risen from a chair and left
the room. At eight o'clock on a Wednesday evening
there was only one place it would have gone, only one
place he and Laurel had gone during the short weeks
he'd known her. It was movie night; surely she remembered.

He hurried over to their place in the park. The sky
was a deep red in the distance, fleeing with the sunset
from the darkness. He scurried breathlessly up the path
and settled his back against the familiar tree. He would
wait. Slowly his runaway breathing returned to him,
and disappeared into the silence.

Golden Gate Park. Where else would you find a
grove of evergreens sprung up from a mound of sand?
He could almost hear Laurel's voice as she laughed and
teased him. Where else could you find windmills and an
old Norwegian sloop with an unpronounceable name,
or a crazy doorway from somebody's old mansion just
standing there in the artificial wilderness beside a lake?
Where else?

He'd have to say he didn't know, and laugh. She

could always get so excited about the most obvious, beautiful things. How did she do it?

Frankie had never been able to do it. He wondered if he ever would. Laurel could make everything she did seem like footprints on the moon. How could she keep that up?

He remembered the time he'd asked her if she loved him. She hadn't answered, but he knew she did. She couldn't hide anything from him. Now if she'd only come. The story could end here—or start here.

It grew dark and Frankie continued his vigil. The traffic fell into line beyond the trees. Pedestrians passed from time to time. The night grew darker and the sky piped forth small silent traces of light, called stars, from the incorporeal distance.

His sense of time disappeared soon enough, with the sunset, and the reliable traffic continued along Lincoln Way. The groups of people, bonded and certified lovers and friends, came and went, talking and gesticulating in an animated fashion. A siren sounded in the distance and the blue light approached and passed. Frankie sat with his back to the rough tree, alone in the moonlight—watching over nothing.

It was the next morning that he saw her. He'd almost adjusted to her absence, in an unsure, jittery sort of way, and was walking rapidly down the sidewalk on the other side of the road from Lopez, when he saw her. He was going early to the game. He carried his own basketball under his right arm, in case the others hadn't come yet. His sneakers were light and his stride quick and sure.

Laurel was in front of Lopez, separated from him by the random cars. She and Pauline were talking to J.T. and laughing. J.T. was going through some kind of elaborate story, talking and waving his hands, and Laurel was eating it up. She was smiling her smile. Frankie could see the sparkle in her eyes from across the street.

He was uncertain at first of what he should do. He could jump the wall and escape into the quiet of the park, but he could not be sure that she hadn't seen him. He could pretend not to have seen her himself and continue walking on his way toward the distant cleft in the wall. Or he could go over. Or he could sneak back the other way. It was a decision of panic. It was no decision at all.

At last she spotted him, accidentally at first, and then decisively. He kept walking, but could not look away. For one long, elaborate moment, they gazed at one another, and they were like two attractive strangers, one on the boat and one on the shore, who know, with a glimpse of melancholy insight, that they will never meet.

When the angle became too great, their eyes parted, and Frankie's numb feet carried him off toward the Prayerbook court.

"You had a phone call, Frankie," his mother said when he'd returned home.

"Oh, yeah? Who was it?"

"She didn't say," called his father from the living room. "I was the one who talked to her and she didn't leave her name."

"Oh."

Frankie walked into the living room and looked toward his father, who was sitting in his patchwork chair. He held a glass of clear liquid in his left hand and had a firm grip on the arm of the chair with his right.

"She said it was very important that she talk to you," he enunciated clearly. "She said she'd call back later."

"But she didn't leave her name?"

"No."

It sounded just like Laurel. He knew her so well in some ways, and so poorly in others.

"Just what is it, Frankie? You having a little problem?"

"No, no. It's nothing."

"Ah, come on. It doesn't sound like nothing to me."

"Yeah, well, it's just one of those things." Frankie attempted a wan smile.

"Women problems, you're always gonna have them," his father said. "You're always gonna have them."

Frankie experienced a vague discomfort with the drift of the conversation, as if he were going to be asked to explain some things for which he had no explanations available.

"What's her name?" his father asked.

Frankie hesitated. He looked at the rug beneath his father's slippers. "Laurel," he said finally, as if he hated to give it up.

"Laurel, that's a nice name."

"Yeah."

"Reminds you of something fresh and green."

"Yeah," Frankie said, and he laughed, sardonically, in spite of himself.

His father paused to drink from his transparent glass. Frankie could see right through the liquid as it passed into his mouth.

"That bad, huh?" said his father, after he'd swallowed and cleaned his lips.

"Nah," said Frankie, whose discomfort had just been transformed into an active restlessness. "It's just one of those things."

"I know. Just one of those things."

His father paused, to prepare himself for speaking.

"So let me tell you what I think, Frankie. I think that you think you're unhappy."

"No, I'm not unhappy."

"You think you're unhappy because somebody *made* you unhappy."

"I'm not unhappy."

"As if happiness were something that somebody *did* to you, something you had no responsibility for. Let me tell you something."

"I'm not unhappy, Dad."

"Let me tell you something. Happiness isn't something that somebody gives to you, it's something you create by yourself. It's not a reaction, it's a . . . an approach. Understand? It's like a small, shiny bubble that each of us carries around with him all the time. All of us with these thin, fragile bubbles of happiness, different sizes, some of them bigger and stronger and rounder, like a fat man's bubble, and others thin and very, very weak, like someone who's scared in the dark.

But all these bubbles are things we make for ourselves, little worlds we create. If we make 'em strong, they can rebound off things like a big ole beach ball. If we let 'em get too weak, why, then we'd better be very, very careful."

All the talk had made him thirsty. He took a slow sip, tasting with his tongue, of the mysterious clear liquid.

"You see what I mean, Frankie?"

Frankie hesitated. "Well . . . sure."

"Okay. So here's what we've got to do. Cultivate your bubble."

"Cultivate your bubble?"

"That's right. Cultivate your bubble."

The way his father was pronouncing the word bubble, it was hard for Frankie to know whether he was being serious or not. Bbbl, no vowels at all. Bbbl. Cultivate your bbbl.

"Build it up," his father continued, and Frankie realized that there was no doubt as to his seriousness. "Make it as strong and bright as you can. Make it so bright it can light up all the dark, sad bbbls all around it."

"A big, bright bubble." Frankie smiled. It snuck out of the side of his mouth and made him feel a rush of warmth in his chest.

"A big, bright bbbl." His father nodded his head solemnly. "That's it, Frankie. That's the secret. That's the thing that we've got to get done. Course, we don't always succeed as well as we might."

"No, guess not."

"We aren't always as strong as we'd like to be."

"No."

"But we keep going, Frankie, we keep going."

Yup, we do, Frankie thought, we do.

"Sometimes good things happen to us, sometimes bad, but we continue, Frankie. don't forget that, we continue."

We continue.

His father fell quickly into a purposive silence. His eyes were no longer on Frankie, or even on his drink, but were directed suddenly toward some spot near the floor on the far side of the room. His face was drawn up into a firm but careless frown, as if he had just discovered something horrible, or something miraculous, and was just that far from understanding what in God's name it all meant.

Frankie's own breath was lost somewhere in his throat. His father's sudden departure, and the strange, half-paralyzed expression on his face, had caught Frankie unprepared. It left him isolated and weak. He felt the soft pressure of his own bubble around him, like something familiar and demented, like some mortally stupid part of himself which had come to suffocate him with kindness.

They remained there, quiet and motionless, during the next moments. Frankie felt his own face being screwed into a frown. There being no time, he might have stood there forever.

His father's deep eyes clouded over, and his eyelids settled down over them like a curtain. Somewhere behind, his father had gone off again, in that quiet, sliding moment, to wherever it was that his dark, solitary journeys led him.

His mother's voice gradually intruded. It was tired, but persistent. It was calling them to supper.

They ate their meal in silence. Frankie rather hoped that Laurel wouldn't call back. There was nothing she could say that he had not seen himself earlier that day. There was nothing she could say to make lighter her week of absence from his life. He didn't want to hear excuses. He didn't want to hear explanations. He didn't want to hear whatever other painful things awaited him at the other end of the line. It would be better if she didn't call. His worst fears, and his most hateful imaginings, were being realized with each minute her call was delayed. And yet it seemed right that it should be so.

But her call was all he could think of.

After supper came the clatter of the dishes and silverware. Frankie didn't help, preferring instead to retire to his room with a fresh, colorful *Sports Illustrated*.

The phone rang at six-thirty.

His mother answered it and Frankie waited, setting the magazine aside on his bed.

But it was for her. It was one of her friends, a professional friend. Frankie peeked through the door and watched his mother sit down next to the phone and light a cigarette. She was smiling.

By the time she got off the phone it was too late, Frankie knew it in his bones. Perhaps she had tried to call, perhaps she hadn't, but he knew she wouldn't then.

He climbed into bed with the magazine and tried to read but couldn't. He lay there for some time with the light on, just holding the magazine up in front of him. His body was lifeless, but his mind was active. He thought of Laurel.

He thought of the times they were alone, and of how good she had made him feel. He thought of her eyes, shining toward him and him alone, while he basked in their glow. He thought of her sweet, small hand, touching him so confidently, so surely. That cruel hand, those cruel eyes.

It was easy and natural for him now to picture her with J.T. in some dark, private night scene. It was easy for him to see what she would do.

But it killed him. It made the knot in his stomach hard and big, like a new, unwanted, parasite organ, like a cancer, eating away at the defenseless mush within. It made him want to shout out his burgeoning frustration.

Instead he tried to subdue it, to block it out of his mind. He remembered the time he and Laurel had spoken of crying, she had been doing some at the time, herself. The reason for her crying he couldn't recall. Some pain, something she might have tried to tell him but couldn't.

He had said he couldn't remember crying, not in the last five years, or eight years. It was a strange thing to say. She probably hadn't believed him, but it was true. Crying was a luxury he had managed to ignore. Among others, most of which he probably didn't even recognize, although Laurel knew. But not crying.

What was crying all about, anyway? The socially

accepted way of feeling sorry for yourself. People cry for themselves, and themselves only, though they may deceive themselves into thinking otherwise. People cry at funerals, why? For the dead guy? Unlikely. If the mourners are religious they must truthfully feel he's better off, and if they're not then they're sure at least that he's no worse off. So why cry?

They're crying for themselves. They'll miss him. Like a child cries when he drops a quarter down the sewer.

They cry at weddings, why? They're remembering their own. The happy couple at hand is only a groaning board for their own remembered joys and afflictions.

They cry at sentimental movies, why? Because they see themselves in the shoes of the bereaved hero or heroine (never the departing character) and experience the feelings they would feel if someone they loved or needed died of leukemia or something. It's another popped balloon. Or a quarter down the sewer.

It wasn't pleasant to think about, but it was true. When you cried, you cried for yourself. Nothing more, nothing less. It was a good thing to remember.

Frankie turned out the light and felt the lump, strong and vibrant, inside of him. His thoughts drifted once again to Laurel and J.T. He couldn't stand to think about them together, and he couldn't force himself not to. It was a long, long time before he finally got to sleep.

On Friday morning he decided to make a call, himself. He called, not Laurel, but Pauline.

"Hi, Frankie."

"Pauline, what's the story? What's the story with Laurel? What's the matter with her?"

"What do you mean, what's the matter with her? She's been trying to call you."

"She has?"

"Sure she has. She's tried a couple of times, and either the line was busy or you weren't there or something else got in the way. And you know it hasn't been easy for her. She's not supposed to even think about you, never mind trying to get in touch with you."

"Well, I don't know."

"And you have no idea how hard she's tried to get in touch with you, even when she was warned not to."

"Yeah, but . . . All she had to do was say something."

"What the hell do you think she's been trying to do? You think she's been doing nothing? You think she doesn't give a shit what happens? Goddamn you, Frankie, just because you can do whatever you want, you don't have to answer to anybody at your house, doesn't mean other people don't. I don't know who the hell you think you are."

"Look, Pauline . . ."

"She tried her best, goddamit, and if you don't like it then the hell with you."

"Pauline . . ."

"But I don't expect you to understand that."

"Pauline, I just . . ."

"Forget it, Frankie, forget it."

And she hung up.

Frankie felt like a piece of horseshit in the middle

of the street. There was no reason he should feel like that, nothing he could comprehend, but the feeling was there nonetheless. The only thing he could think was that you could never quite tell just what it was that was going on in other people's heads. It was such a mystery.

He went out shortly after that, to the Prayerbook court, and he came back late. There had been, of course, no call.

His father was drunk by the time he got home, passed out softly in his cushioned chair. His mother was out. He fixed himself something to eat and ate it alone, at the kitchen table. Tonight was the night of Billy Lyons' latest caper. Deep inside he knew he wanted absolutely no part of it. Yet, in quite another way, it seemed the perfect reply to a world which had let him down. Whatever his motivation, he went out after supper to meet Billy, who would be waiting at Lopez.

"It's all set, Frankie. Ralphie's got the truck, man, and things are ready to go."

"Okay."

"Let's make it out to Telegraph Hill, man, okay? Check out the scene of the crime."

"Okay, let's go."

By the time they got out there it was dark. There were cars parked with their grilles at the rim of the circular driveway, but these were still the sightseers, not the lovers. Frankie and Billy had stopped to buy a couple of pints of cheap port on the way. They sat on the wall facing the Bay and drank from the screwtop bottles.

"Well, this is the spot," said Billy.

"Yup, here it is."

The spot, to be exact, was about twenty yards behind them, at the point where the narrow winding road emerged from the trees before spreading out, like a macadam tablecloth, at the top of the hill. Frankie and Billy sat at the table's edge, their legs hanging over the wall, drinking and staring at the sleeping cargo ships and ocean liners that were nestled into quays on the other side of the Embarcadero. The cities of Oakland and Berkeley pulsed weakly in the distance.

"So, listen, man," Billy leaned over to say. "I'll tell you something. You got to get the credit. You got to get the credit."

"Me?" Frankie laughed. "*I* get the credit?"

"Bet your ass you do. You got the idea, you came up with it first. That's all it took, a little cooperative thinking, but it was your idea that was selected."

His idea. So was he the one who was really responsible for this? What was it they were going to do, anyhow? Dump a load of concrete on a roadway.

Frankie had a momentary glimpse into the reason why people do things. They do them because they plan to do them. It gives them something to do while waiting for their lives to end. It fills up the days with a succession of day-filling events. And they all seem so important if you could just concentrate solely on each event, and keep busy, and make sure you don't get inactive or bored, but keep planning, and smiling, and filling up those days. Good God, he thought, that can't be all there is to it? There's got to be some underlying structure to the whole thing. It can't be that pointless. How can human beings who have built cathedrals be satisfied with datebooks and filling up their days?

But how much more than that were he and Billy doing, sitting there on the wall and waiting for their next event?

Frankie was restless. "Hey, Billy, let's take a walk or something."

"Why?"

"I don't know, but maybe we shouldn't be sitting here like this."

"Why not?"

"Well, I mean, sitting here drinking wine and looking conspicuous. Somebody might see us and remember."

Billy dismissed it with a wave of his hand. "So what, man, forget it. First of all, nobody ever looks twice at two people sitting up here drinking wine. What could be more natural than that? Second, even if they did, what does that prove? It only proves we were drinking wine, not dumping concrete. Shit, it's even an alibi. How could we be out getting concrete to dump if we're up here all night getting shitfaced?"

That sounded reasonable.

"Just relax, Frankie. Hey, dig it, man, tonight's the night. The caper. All we got to do now is wait."

Tonight's the night, Frankie thought, the event. Just like the businessmen and the patrons of the arts, at least it gives us something to do. "What time's Ralphie supposed to get here again?"

"Quarter of twelve."

"Well, that gives us about three hours."

"Yeah, well, what the hell. We'll take our time."

They took their time.

Billy renewed the conversation, off-handedly enough. "You still making it with that chick from L.A.?"

"Oh, I don't know. Not too much lately."

"How come?"

"I don't know. Just haven't felt like it."

"Oh. You know, you ought to cut down on your basketball or something. I hear too much of that shit can make you sterile."

"Bullshit. It just makes you bigger."

He laughed. "Yeah, big and limp."

Frankie drank from his bottle and felt the warmth in his chest. He and Billy had always got along so well. It was all so natural; he never felt he had to put up his guard, he could just say whatever it was that came to his mind. Billy always laughed at his jokes and Frankie always thought Billy's were funny. It was just a natural collusion. He was the kind of person Frankie felt he could have talked to about Laurel, or about The Shadow, and felt confident that his statements would have been taken at their face value, and not as the bizarre intrusions or tasteless embarrassments for which most of his friends would have taken them. It was a pleasant feeling of comradeship. It was so reassuring that it made the actual bringing up of these topics unnecessary.

They quietly drank their wine and looked at the Bay. The only sound was a low moan which came from the direction of the water. It was like the sound of the ocean, itself. The dark, deep, fish-cold ocean.

Frankie glanced out toward the Golden Gate. Somewhere out there beyond the fantastic wide horizon strange foreign ships cut ploddingly through the dark ocean, the wine-dark sea. What would it be like to be among them, to be a lost, nameless sailor on the wine-dark sea? Sailing out into the unknown. Searching for . . . something, new uncharted lands or something. Something to discover, although the romance was only in the searching.

He took a nice deep draft of wine, and the sound of his swallowing left behind it a soft calm to surround his reverie. All the plodding ships, churning across the wine-dark sea.

It must have been going on forever, all that movement.

It must have been something, in the old days, a thousand years ago, in those unlit, barren days, when boys and men sat at the edge of a continent and longed to sail out into the wide, rolling darkness. Weak, determined ships, with painted sails and toothpick oars, setting out into the teeth of danger. Women, beautiful heroic women, awaiting their return. While the wooden prows of the ships sheared through the night into the dawn.

It must have been something.

Billy was nudging him with his elbow. "Frankie, dig it, let's get some more wine."

Frankie looked at his bottle and saw the last of the dark liquid, flashing in the moonlight.

"Whaddya say?" Billy prodded.

Frankie smiled. "Okay."

"And, hey, I got another idea, man. There's no sense wasting *all* our time up here—let's get the wine and take in a skin flick down on Broadway." Frankie held out his empty bottle with two fingers, and dropped it unceremoniously down into the scrub pine on the side of Telegraph Hill. "Why not?"

They had their pints of wine under their jackets and they drifted into the theater just as the feature was about to start. There were twenty or thirty moviegoers scattered throughout the screening room when they arrived. Most were men, older and alone; they looked like small, nervous islands wrapped in raincoats.

Billy chose an aisle and slid immediately all the way in to the center, where he sat at the elbow of a solitary patron, who became extremely uncomfortable. Billy looked at him and smiled; the fellow looked quickly away. Undaunted, Billy leaned toward him and proffered his newly opened bottle of port.

"Care for some?"

The fellow gathered up his raincoat and left. Billy and Frankie were left by themselves in the middle of the theater, like a small, dry atoll in a sea of masturbation. Huddling together, they watched the film.

It was called *Dr. Heisenberg's Magic Eyes* and it was about this fat, greasy guy who found he could see through clothes and things. Naturally he began to use his newfound talent in predictable fashion, peering into girls' locker rooms, bedrooms, etc. Or else he'd stand on the street corner like some foreign disease and watch with drooling interest as the beautiful girls popped into nakedness while walking briskly down the street. It was a funny, and rather shoddy, technical shift from a prim green tweed suit to bright nakedness and a shapely ass winking provocatively away from the camera. The audience loved it, Frankie could tell by their raincoats.

While Dr. Heisenberg peered into various situations, Frankie gulped his wine until, shortly, the glow in his throat spread to his whole body. He was loaded. Peacefully loaded.

Billy leaned over. "Hey, look at that."

Frankie looked and saw Dr. Heisenberg peeking through a side door into a nursing home. The patients padded about, all old and withered, with breasts like dry prunes, and purple veins, and all their skin shrinking back through every orifice toward some vengeful center of their bodies. It made Frankie think of a poem by T. S. Eliot, not too surprising an occurrence, given his lack of sobriety.

. . . And saw the skull beneath the skin.

Billy put his hand over his eyes and said, "That's disgusting."

That made Frankie laugh. "What's disgusting? Old people?"

"No. Showing them like that, that's disgusting."

Frankie laughed and shook his head. "Senior citizen porn."

"Well, I can't get off on that."

Frankie raised a finger and whispered, "Someday you will."

Billy smiled back in recognition. "Yeah, well, I can wait."

Meanwhile, Dr. Heisenberg watched the naked old people for a short while longer, until a plump, young, giant-nippled nurse came into the room, and he watched her.

"Seriously, though," Billy whispered, "how would you like to be able to do that? See right through clothes like that?"

"I don't know. You'd probably get used to it."

"Yeah, but it'd be quite a show for a while."

"I guess so. It'd be fun."

"You could shock a few people, too. Like you meet a chick on the bus, she's with her parents or something. You say, 'Hey there, sweetheart, how's it going? Still got that birthmark next to your nipple?' Blow their minds."

"Blow their minds."

"*You* know she's got the birthmark, you can see it. Her parents know it, they're her parents. She doesn't know you from Adam, but I'd like to see her convince her parents she doesn't."

"Right, right."

Frankie wouldn't have thought of that gag in a million years. He wouldn't even have thought to think of a gag. It'd be too embarrassing; better to be inconspicuous if you're peeking through girls' clothes.

"Or how about this one?" Billy whispered again. " 'Hi, baby, hey, I heard you shaved the hair off your snatch.' She'd turn a beautiful red and head for her boyfriend to see who the hell he's been talking to."

"Right."

"And, dig it, look, the bastard can see through venetian blinds, too."

Indeed he could, and he was proving it at that very moment by standing outside a motel room and peering through the drawn blinds. The inhabitants of the room obliged him by having an orgy.

There were four of them, two men, two women. Both the men were paunchy and wore black socks. The women wore nothing at all. One of the women was older, with teased black hair and lipstick. Her pubic hair was stringy and thin. But it was the other girl who drew Frankie's attention; she didn't look like she belonged there at all. She was young, she could have been close to Frankie's age. She was small and blond and clean-looking, like a high school girl. Her eyes were clear, not heavy lidded and obvious like the other's. There must have been some mistake. Why was she there?

They all began doing things soon enough and one of the two fat, greasy old men was on top of her and pumping away at her. Frankie felt the knot in his chest. He drank wine to relieve it but it didn't help. Instead his stomach gurgled and his head rang.

The girl was lying there with her face toward the camera and her eyes closed. Frankie couldn't read her face, but it was clear that she wasn't enjoying it. The fat, greasy slob heaved and plunged with his moist, flabby face and lips hovering over her. She endured it. Why was she there? How had they convinced her to do it?

She looked like a high school girl; she didn't need
to be there. Somebody should have told her.
Her lips pouted from time to time, and Frankie
could see her front teeth, tight against her lower lip. Her
face was thin and fresh, and her body was brand-new,
a soft jewel. He couldn't see, he couldn't understand it.
They changed partners then, with the other fat guy
shuffling over to Frankie's blonde. He had an unintelligible tattoo on his biceps, and his penis stuck out, slick
and long, in front of him. Frankie felt so weak and
saddened by the whole thing. The wine rumbled in his
stomach like lava in a volcano.

The blond girl looked so pale and small standing
next to him. Her face was quiet, with only a hint of the
cardboard smile which was required by the camera.
They stood for a short time, while she masturbated him
with her hand, before she knelt slowly down before him
and took him directly into her mouth.

Frankie was going to be sick; it was the wine.

"Billy, gotta split."

"What's the matter?"

"Don't feel good."

"I'll come with you."

"No, meetcha later, meetcha later."

He scooted quickly out of the theater and threw up
on the sidewalk. People tried not to notice as they
passed.

Frankie walked around for a while, to clear his
head. He drank from the rest of his wine to wash the
taste of the vomit from his mouth. He still felt extremely

shaky. He wasn't staggering or anything, but inside he felt extremely shaky. Not to mention screwed up.

After a while he began to realize that it was getting late, and that he'd have to think about meeting Billy and Ralphie at a quarter to twelve. But he was still too drunk and confused to care properly about any meeting or engagement he might have made. He just didn't care.

It was when he found himself on Montgomery Street, and the only pedestrian in the area at that time, that the idea of calling Laurel entered his head. Just like that, as if it had snuck up behind him and gone *Boo.* Her father might be home, it was probably too late, he didn't know what he would say, or what she might think—but he just didn't care. He just didn't care.

The light in the phone booth clicked on when he shut the squeaking doors. He dropped the dime into the slot and waited for the two bells. Then he dialed her number. 555–8404.

A male voice answered at the other end of the line. "Hello?"

Her father.

Frankie made a stab at speech. "Hlo?"

"Hello?"

"'S Laurel there?"

"Who is this?"

"Uhm. 'S Laurel there?"

"No she's not. Now who is this?"

Pause.

"Is this Frankie O'Day?"

Pause.

"Okay, Frankie, I know it's you. Laurel's not here,

she's with her mother at Lake Tahoe and she'll be up there for the rest of the summer, so you might as well forget about her."

"Oh."

"And I just want you to know, I think it was a pretty rotten thing you did the other night, and if that's the kind of boy you are you can forget about seeing Laurel again, ever."

"I dinn do it."

"What?"

Frankie tried to force his lips and tongue to talk.

"I—dinnt—do it."

"Oh, come on now, what kind of a jerk do you take me for? I know you were the one. Who else could it have been? Instead of trying to slither your way out of it, you might try straightening up a little. You messed up this time, but if you can pull yourself together maybe you'll be all right in the future. What in hell's the matter with you, anyway?"

"Urnh," Frankie grunted.

"Well, I'll tell you one damn thing's the matter with you, you're too young, too goddamn young to be drinking like that. Don't you know better than that?"

"Mmna."

"Well you'd better learn. Jesus Christ, I'd think that with your father's situation you'd know better."

Silence. The phone line crackled and the wind blew past the phone booth.

"Well, good night," Mr. Travers said. He waited a perfunctory moment and hung up the phone. Only the wind continued.

Frankie was alone in the vacant quiet. His head felt warm and his ears rang with a distant, muffled chime. He was still drunk, and his insides felt washed away, as if by the wine.

Working its way slowly through the sponge that was his head, a melancholy echo rose in his ears. "I'd think that with your father's situation you'd know better."

—Your father's situation—
—You'd know better—
—Your father's situation—
—You'd know better—

Frankie was extremely tired. It was an effort to return the receiver to its cradle. He leaned against the glass side of the phone booth and opened the doors just enough to turn out the light. He remained there for a long time, staring at the darkened entrance to a building across the street. Whatever went on in there during the day, it was silent and lifeless at night. The gray stone just stood there, matching its stolid permanence against the slow hours. It seemed impossible that it would not win.

After a while there was a furtive activity near the corner of the building. One shadow, appearing out of nowhere and suddenly there, facing the wall. Its movements seemed pointless: turning, bending, standing. At last it stood straight and raised its arm toward the wall. Its hand held a small spray can, and it left behind it a dark stain on the ash-colored wall. Frankie knew before it started writing what the word would be. He also knew, by the sweatshirt with the familiar number, who it was that was laboring in the darkness.

When the word was finished, and the figure with the spray can was preparing to go, Frankie stepped out of the phone booth. He intended to do so quietly, but the squeak of the doors came unnaturally loud in the deserted street. The figure froze momentarily, then turned toward Frankie. The face flashed from a reflection in the secret darkness like an apparition. His eyes stared toward him for a moment, and then vanished.

Frankie stumbled to the trolley, and home, and to bed.

PART

Swirling fragments. Bird noises. Children. The dry, dry air.

Sleep.

Bright white morning room, there and oppressive just beyond the sticky leaden eyelids. Something ringing like a sprung clock in the internal distance. Phantom dreams of pineapple juice just left behind.

Back to the strange kitchen. He'd been getting a cold cool drink from the frosty smooth gallon. Pouring it into the tall wet glass. Ice cubes, get ice cubes. Piles of ice cubes in the freezer. Cold and wet against the all-pervading dryness. Cold and wet.

The kitchen was a room surrounded by doors, with one old-fashioned wooden table in the middle. Its top was maple brown and the finish had been worn away by years of use. One bare light bulb hung in neglect from the ceiling. The one window looked out into a brown and green-gray broken-down-fence skid-row jungle. One bottle in the refrigerator, waiting, full of grapefruit juice.

Drink, goddamit, drink and drink and drink.

From behind the doors came sounds of sleeping. Bodies sleeping like death behind the doors. He wanted to wake them up but he didn't know who was there and was afraid. It was as if he were in a movie which skipped like a record. He went back and back again to the refrigerator to pour out the cool refreshing liquid but he didn't drink. He just kept going back and pouring.

Drink!

But he kept on pouring, pouring, until he couldn't breathe anymore. His mouth had crusted over, like an abandoned riverbed in the hot sun. Meanwhile, all the others went on sleeping. Behind their doors.

He opened his eyes to a blast of white air and the dream left him. He covered his head with the swirl of sheet and blanket and thought of grapefruit juice. There must be some.

Bird noises came. And the silly little *putt-putt*

sounds of the cars. From somewhere behind him came the faint *clang-clang* of the N Judah as it slid out toward the beach. It felt like Saturday. The sun must have been bright and he just knew he'd have to get up for some grapefruit juice, but he put his arms up over his eyes and tried not to move.

More noises. Kids in the street. Short, high-pitched kid noises from the street. Playing a Saturday-morning game.

Here we go round the grizzly bear
Grizzly bear, grizzly bear
Here we go round the grizzly bear
So early in the morning

Here we go round the grizzly bear
Grizzly bear, grizzly bear
Here we go round the grizzly bear
So early in the morning

Over and over again. The kids outside, with the grizzly bear. He could picture them, in a bright, childish circle, hand in hand, dancing back and forth around a tall, dark, stupid bear. Smiling and skipping in a circle until, gradually, their demeanor changed, and the whole situation changed, and it was no longer smiling and dancing but leering and laughing, and the maddening noise left the bear sick and confused and swiping hopelessly, like King Kong on the Empire State Building at the toy planes that taunted him and sought to bring him down. The planes darted by, one after another, until the giant creature grabbed his chest in pain, holding for one final minute against the inevitable, before falling, time suspended, to his death in the streets below.

Mercifully, the children stopped their chant and went on to another game. Frankie struggled from his bed and staggered toward the kitchen. Seriously wounded in his own way, he could think only of the aspirin and grapefruit juice that would save him.

The road to the Prayerbook court was paved with ghosts. People he'd once known and things they'd said. He also felt very dry and somewhat displaced, despite the gigantic, almost gluttonous breakfast he'd eaten. Nothing made much sense.

As he came around the trees toward the court he could see that the game was in progress. As if it had always been there. Number 44 was there, dancing up and down the court like a salmon in the cool, familiar water.

Frankie thought of the red-scrawled calls to action on surfaces of the city. Action. Red splotches in the arid wasteland. Action.

It looked as if 44 saw him coming and lost control of the ball on purpose. It slipped off his fingers and came rolling toward Frankie, who scooped it up and held it out in front of him as he approached the court. Number 44 jogged right up to him and took it out of his hands.

"Hey, man," Frankie stopped and greeted him softly, smiling.

Number 44 looked back at him with eyes commanding him to be silent.

"Hey, look, I'm not gonna tell anyone."

"Just don't wreck it now," the kid whispered.

"I'm not gonna wreck it."

"Just don't."

"I won't, man. Not me."

Frankie shuffled his feet, then looked back up, with one last question. "Hey, look, just tell me, what do you mean by it, action, what kind of action you talking about?"

The kid looked at him with astonishment. "It's not just any fucking kind of action, Jim, not just *any*thing."

"What kind is it then?"

The kid shook his head. "Oh, wow, man, if I gotta tell you then you might as well hang it up anyway."

"Yeah," Frankie said. Action. "Don't worry, man, I won't wreck it."

The kid peered into his eyes; it was like a test of endurance and integrity. Frankie held on to his eyes as if he were holding his own capricious integrity in check. The kid turned away, satisfied, and went back to the game. The sun glided slowly across the sky and carried away the afternoon, high above the basketball games and picnics and rowboats, toward its destination somewhere beyond the Prayerbook Cross.

It was gray and quiet in the twilight as he walked home. The cars on Lincoln Way seemed to travel on a blanket of air, timidly, with their headlights shining weakly in the thickening dusk. They say it's the time of day which is most difficult for the driver, when he sometimes sees things that aren't there, or when he fails to see those that are.

Frankie ignored the cars and walked quickly along

the cracked sidewalk. Next to him the old crumbling wall ran, separating him from the park. He passed the hill where he and Laurel had spent their evenings, a place that had meant so much to him, but he could produce no emotion for it now. He peeked through the trees to the soft top of the hillock and saw only that it was empty, that there was no one there.

It was over, really. There was no sense kidding yourself. The whole thing with Laurel must have been ill-starred from the first, if only he had known. If only there were any possible way to know such things. But they were hidden. They remained hidden, life's small mysteries.

It was over.

He passed Lopez Market, the place where they'd first met, and he didn't even bother to give it a glance.

Just as he was prepared to cross the street, heading home, a figure approached out of the falling shadow. It was an arresting apparition, and not for any obvious characteristic, but only for its hint of some unresolved confusion, some secret ambiguity in its makeup. The figure walked quickly, with short movements of its legs only, and held its slender trunk erect. Its arms were folded across its chest, in the manner that girls affect so easily, but its long legs were male. As the lineaments of the figure grew more pronounced, Frankie saw the pale face, with its high, strong cheekbones, its penciled eyebrows, and its dyed gossamer hair. As the figure walked by, it smiled, with its lips tightly compressed, and its eyes followed him in their sockets until Frankie thought they might slide completely out of its head, and fall, wet and inconsolable, to the pavement below.

It made him shiver. His breath came back slowly as he hurried across the highway.

Once he'd safely reached the familiar corner of his street, he turned and watched the figure as it receded into the twilight. A queen, heading toward the beach. Frankie shook his head; it was a mystery.

Everything was a mystery, lately, for God's sake. There was no counting on anything; nothing seemed reliable. Even your sex could change from day to day. People could come and go, enter and leave, but the only thing that would remain the same would be the mysterious peephole through which you watched your life, and the people in it, pass. It was hardly a reassuring certainty.

Frankie headed slowly home. His legs felt slow and easy, his sneakers soft on the sidewalk.

You hardly knew where to start. Never mind where you were going. It seemed like they'd taken away all the old heroic things, the things that made your heart pump faster and brought tears of empathy to your eyes. Maybe somewhere there existed a small, heroic pocket of life, somewhere in the desert maybe, in a valley of pueblo cliff dwellings or somewhere. A place where everyone got up in the morning and knew what they were there for and the sun was shining bright orange on the warm mesa.

A place that wasn't likely to exist.

What you were left with instead was the here and now, which perhaps existed, although you probably couldn't count on it. In the old days there might have been heroes, struggling mightily in a battle with life, but no more. Today there was no way to tell just what in the world you were supposed to struggle against. Or for.

Instead of heroes today you have nuts and mass murderers who at least have some sort of warped idea of what life is supposed to be about. Or you have movie stars and professional athletes to model your life after, which is like trying to imitate a loaf of bread. In the final event you have to make do with yourself. Cultivate your bubble maybe.

As he walked up the stairs he thought how quickly Laurel Travers had come and gone in his life, so quickly that she might not have been there at all, a trick of the imagination. But he still felt numb when he thought of her, and there was a part of him, deep inside, which was incredibly saddened by their inability to really mean anything to each other. That knot in his stomach which he'd carried so long in her absence was gone, but there was an empty spot now where it had been. Something was missing. It wasn't something to cry about, but he felt sad and—numb.

As he entered the house he heard his mother's voice rising loud and agitated from the darkened living room. She was yelling something at his father; they must have been arguing. Frankie slipped past without their seeing. He didn't want to walk in on their argument. He went to his room instead.

The walls were not thick and the sound of his mother's voice came through, in short phrases. His father seemed to make no answer to her questions.

"What did you expect?

"What did you expect me to do?

"You think it's easy?

"You think I don't feel beaten down sometimes, too?

"You think I don't wish I could escape it all sometimes, too?

"You think I don't feel like just jumping off a cliff or something sometimes?

"You think I don't feel like that?

"Do you think I have any feelings at all?

"Do you?

"For God's sake, *say* something. Do you?

"Do you?

"Do you?

"Sometimes I just can't stand it anymore, you know that? I just can't stand it.

"Why don't you say something? Say anything, just don't sit there, talk."

Her voice died away, as if from fatigue. Finally she left the room and went to her study. She closed the door softly behind her.

The house became still and quiet, as if everyone were suddenly sleeping. From out of the silence came the small house sounds: the refrigerator motor and the muffled cackle of a distant television set. Beneath his feet the floor felt spongy and uncertain.

Despite an internal injunction to leave things alone, Frankie returned to his door and opened it. The sound of the television came a bit louder, more definite, from the living room. There was no other sound.

He waited, then walked slowly, as if in a dream, around the corner and into the living room, where his father was.

The cold light of the television flickered and made shadows jump in an otherwise dark room. His father was in his chair. On TV was a religious program, a preacher in a conservative suit and tie standing in a pulpit and leading a humble congregation in prayer. His father's head was thrown carelessly back and to the side, his mouth open and his breathing regular and childlike. He looked so small and vulnerable there, in a way Frankie had never noticed before. Like a child. The preacher and his flock were reciting the Our Father, with first his voice speaking a phrase, then the entire rumbling congregation repeating it. Their sterile light fell on his father's face and it seemed at once as if they were reciting it all for him, as if his father were the mortally damaged child, so sweetly sleeping, who was so unreasonably destined to be taken from them. He must have been sleeping for hours; he was innocent of everything. Frankie felt the red rim of tears forming at the corners of his eyes. Slowly it merged with the scene in front of him and carried them both, for a time, away. Behind him the nervous, shuffling mourners continued.

For Thine is the kingdom

For Thine is the kingdom

And the power

And the power

And the glory

And the glory

Forever and ever

Forever and ever.

Amen.

Format by Ellen Weiss
Set in 12/14 Times Roman
Composed by The Haddon Craftsmen, Inc.
Printed by The Book Press
Bound by The Book Press
HARPER & ROW, PUBLISHERS, INC.